THE HALF
ROUTE

Halfway, But Never Halfhearted

Dr. Kishor Kumar Attal

Disclaimer

This is a work of fiction. Names, characters, places, institutions and events are either the product of the author's imagination or are used fictitiously. Any resemblance of any kind to any actual person living or dead, events, incidents and places entirely confidential. The publisher and the author will not be responsible for any action taken by reader based on the content of this book. This work does not aim to hurt the sentiments of any religion, nationality, class, sect, region or gender.

The Half Route

"Halfway, But Never Halfhearted"

Mail: author.kishorattal@gmail.com
Website: www.kishorattal.com
Genre: Fiction

Acknowledgements

The decision to write The Half Route came to me when I realized that this story needed to be narrated. I am sincerely thankful to my daughter "Ashtami Shree" for all her valuable inputs and my son Jaisal Singh, for his support. I would also like to thank Maata ji (my mother-in- law Smt. Rajkumari) for her unwavering support throughout the years.

Many thanks to the companies and managers I've worked with over the years. They gave me the chance to go to the numerous places around the world and have the experiences that I have been talked about in this book. It was a beautiful adventure.

While working on The Half Route, I began to realise that writing isn't a solitary task as we are led to believe. There are editors, proofreaders, and of course publishers involved in the whole process.

To me, it has been a truly rewarding experience. I would like to sincerely thank you, my readers, for picking up this book and giving this story a chance.

Prologue

When Karan was born, his fate had already been determined – he would become an engineer. It's always been decreed as such, especially in a then developing country like India. Your career choices are limited. During Karan's growing up years, the best of students always became doctors, lawyers, and engineers. Careers in arts and other subjects were almost unheard of!

In fact, it wouldn't be until well into the late 2000s that the internet would take over everyone's lives and a whole new industry would crop up. Writers were rare and far between. Successful writers were a rarer phenomenon. Art went hand-in-hand with the image of a starving artist.

As he traveled around the world, helping bring different constructions to life, the last thing that he thought he would do was tell the story. He didn't think that he would be sitting down to put his thoughts together, put them down in pen and paper, and eventually hold the final product in the form of a book!

Through his life's experiences Karan would come to learn that everyone's story is truly unique and that the stories need to be told. While he had readily gone with the flow of life's plan that had been presented to him from the moment he was born, he was lucky enough to live at a time when he witnessed firsthand the changes. It made him determined to tell the story to the world.

He had seen enough of life to know that he needed to tell the stories. Because someone out there would use it as their survival guide. There is no point in keeping our experiences and our hardships to ourselves. When you share your happiness and your successes, that happiness is multiplied. When you share the hardships and your sorrows, the sadness decreases, for we will never know what's going on with another person (as we'll learn later on as this story progresses as well), until we actually bother to sit down and ask them what's going on.

Given the increasing amount of people who chose to live abroad without their families just to provide them with a better life, Karan believed there would be more people who resonated with his stories. More people would benefit if they knew about all the things he had gone through. And of course, the added bonus, they would learn about the different countries and continents that he had visited over the course of his life.

From dodging landmines in Afghanistan to sharing his private space with wild animals in Africa to being taken aback by the hospitality in North Africa – Karan's journey spans decades and continents. Some of his experiences feel straight out of the storybooks. And some of them feel like they need to be told to generations to come so that they remember what it's like to live through these situations.

So, Karan sat down, gathered his thoughts, and wrote the story of how he had lived since he graduated from college and got a job.

And, thus was born The Half Route – the book that you are currently holding in your hands.

About the Author

Dr. Kishor Kumar Attal, born and raised in Delhi, India, comes from a middle-class background and currently serves as an Executive Director of Operations in the construction industry.

His illustrious career has taken him to over 48 countries for work and travel, where he has managed and delivered prestigious projects across India, Afghanistan, Central Asia, Africa, the Gulf, Middle Eastern countries, Russia, East European countries and beyond.

Dr. Attal holds both India Book and Asia Book records for his extraordinary speed in project completion. In addition to his professional success, he is an avid rifle shooter and a book enthusiast.

Inspired by his global experiences, he has recently turned to writing. His novel introduces Mr. Karan, a character who navigates complex personal and professional challenges, embodying themes of resilience and transformation.

Table of Contents

CHAPTER - ONE

In India, they tell you what you have to do the minute you are born. Go to school. Study hard. Be one of the toppers. Choose science or maybe commerce. But Science is what you should stick to. Then become either a doctor or engineer. That's what the smart kids always do. But smart kids are not told many things.

For example: in the labyrinth of post-completion of education life in India, many find themselves grappling with the harsh reality of limited job opportunities and the pressure to settle for less. For individuals like Karan, born and raised amidst the bustling streets of New Delhi, in the heart of a middle-class family, Karan's journey began without the guiding hand of privilege or mentorship. From the labyrinthine alleys of his childhood to the sprawling classrooms of academia, he charted his course alone, fueled by an unyielding determination to grasp the elusive promise of higher education, particularly in the realm of engineering technology. who have diligently pursued their studies only to encounter a dearth of satisfactory employment options, the journey from disillusionment to determination is a challenging one.

He knew he had done the right thing by selecting Construction technology. How was he supposed

to know that despite having a prestigious degree once he was out of college he would be greeted

with a new problem?

Too many technical aspects, and not enough projects. He chose the right line of construction field just at a very, very wrong time! Having completed his education with high hopes and aspirations, Karan was eager to embark on a career path that would not only utilize his skills but also provide a sense of fulfillment.

However, the harsh reality of the job market soon dawned upon him—satisfactory jobs were

few and far between, and competition was fierce. After months of fruitless searching, Karan found himself faced with a difficult decision—to accept a job offer that fell far short of his expectations or continue his search in the hopes of landing a more prestigious position with a handsome salary.

Because he had to make ends meet, he decided to go ahead with the first job he landed. The salary was nothing to write home about. But he decided that something was better than nothing – and this was just a stepping stone in the road. He was sure his luck would turn soon.

And he was right.

His father is a contractor. Back then, during one of his major projects, he took Karan to the office of one of his clients since he needed some measurements to be done. The chairman, who also happened to be his father's friend, asked his father, about the measurements being presented to him. He was delighted to learn that it was Karan, his father's son, who had demonstrated such skills.

"There is a project," the Chairman said, "it's in Afghanistan and we need someone with your skillset on the ground. If you have a passport, would you be willing to go there?"

Karan, soon learned that the project was building a highway from Afghanistan to Faizabad, Pakistan. The salary he was offering was many times higher than what he was currently making at the office job he had.

To him, it was a no-brainer. He leaped at the opportunity.

Without much deliberation, he announced to his family, "A job opportunity has presented itself in Afghanistan. I will be moving there for some time. I hope you will support me in my endeavors – because I am undertaking this opportunity to ensure we have a better quality of life."

His family gave him their support unconditionally. Soon, his bags were packed and he was headed on a one-way ticket to a war-ravaged country, to help make it better. Little did Karan know then that this would be the beginning of all of his travel tales.

Afghanistan would become the first of many places that he would travel to for work purposes.

***

In the project in Afghanistan, he had been assigned as a Site Engineer. Working there was completely different from what it's like working back home in India. Today, if his team fails to deliver the agreed-upon work, they would be reprimanded. But there, they were working on the highway, in between literally fighting for their lives.

He had been explicitly informed by the supervisors that since the World Bank had granted permission to hire twenty engineers, they needed to show the paperwork for twenty engineers on the project. They didn't keep a tab on how much work was getting achieved every day. Their only target was to reach the base camp by 4.30 PM. Even a five-minute delay would result in the German soldiers, who were providing them with protection, to go out and look for them. Reaching the camp by 4.30 PM was absolutely non-negotiable! He realized that the priorities for projects in each country would be different. In India, it's meeting your targets. In Afghanistan, it was keeping yourself alive!

This bureaucratic requirement was non-negotiable, emphasizing the importance of compliance with administrative protocols. Despite this focus on paperwork, there was a notable lack of daily oversight of the actual progress being made. The supervisors did not meticulously monitor how much work was being achieved on a day-to-day basis.

Their primary and singular objective each day was to ensure that all team members reached the base camp by 4:30 PM without fail. This deadline was strictly enforced, as even a delay of five minutes would prompt the German soldiers, who were tasked with providing protection for the team, to initiate a search operation. The punctual arrival at the camp by 4:30 PM was not merely a guideline but an absolute mandate, underscoring the critical nature of their safety protocols.

This rigid adherence to the 4:30 PM deadline highlighted the stark reality of working in a volatile and dangerous environment. The presence of the German soldiers, assigned to protect the team, underscored the ever-present risk and the necessity of strict time management to ensure their safety. The soldiers' readiness to embark on a search mission at the slightest delay illustrated the precariousness of their situation and the high stakes involved. The daily race to reach the base camp on time became a symbol of the broader challenges they faced, where administrative procedures and survival were tightly interwoven.

"This is troublesome," Karan thought to himself, "Even if there's a five-minute worth of work left, we have to clock out at 4.30 PM, no questions asked. There's no question of stretching ourselves!"

He couldn't very well argue with the German soldiers stationed there to help him and his team get back to the base camp safely. Karan found himself thinking about the differences between how he had handled projects before and now. Years later, he would still think about his time in Afghanistan and how different it had been from the other times we had worked around the world.

Through these experiences, he came to a profound realization about the varying priorities of projects depending on the country and its unique circumstances. In India, the primary focus of project management often revolved around meeting targets and adhering to deadlines. The success of a project was measured by its ability to achieve set goals within the stipulated time frame, reflecting a structured and goal-oriented approach. Conversely, in Afghanistan, the overriding priority was starkly different. In this war-torn and unpredictable environment, the paramount concern was ensuring personal safety and staying alive amidst the constant threat of violence and instability. The contrast between these two contexts was striking, shedding light on the diverse challenges and priorities that define project management in different parts of the world.

***

When Karan left for this project, his son was three years old and his daughter was just two

months old. Even though he knew the risk he was putting himself in, Karan was determined to

come back alive. It took him a good couple of months to be at ease in the base camp.

As Karan embarked on his journey to the project site in Afghanistan, his son's laughter still echoed in his mind, a tender reminder of the little boy he left behind, barely three years old,

and his daughter, a mere two months old, cradled in the arms of his wife.

"Come back home to us safely," his wife had told him. "I'll keep you in my prayers."

His son was too young to understand his father would be gone for a while. So, he had simply given him a hug and wished him a goodbye. In the child's mind, his father might have just stepped out to get vegetables from the market! Karan didn't have the heart to explain to him that it would be a while until they saw each other again.

Despite the weight of responsibility and the looming specter of danger, Karan harbored a fierce resolve to return to his family unscathed, a silent promise etched into the fabric of his being. Yet, as he acclimated to the rugged rhythms of life in the Afghan base camp, it wasn't merely the passage of time, but a gradual surrender to the harsh embrace of his surroundings that finally granted him a semblance of peace.

In the rugged terrain of Afghanistan, where danger lurks around every corner and the threat of violence looms large, the safety of personnel working on-site is paramount. The harsh environment is not only physically demanding but also fraught with security challenges that are unlike any he had encountered before. The unpredictable nature of the landscape, combined with the constant risk posed by insurgent activities, creates a uniquely perilous setting for those tasked with developmental and engineering projects. As an engineer navigating this treacherous landscape, he found himself surrounded by a team of security guards armed to the teeth with modern weaponry, tasked with ensuring his safety from the ever-present threat of Taliban insurgents. The presence of these guards was a constant reminder of the volatile and dangerous environment in which they operated, underscoring the critical importance of security measures.

With six to eight security guards equipped with an array of deadly weapons, including wagons and rocket launchers, he embarked on his daily duties with a sense of both gratitude and apprehension. The guards' arsenal was not just a precaution but a necessary response to the level of threat they faced daily. Escort vehicles accompanied their movements, forming a protective convoy designed to deter any potential attacks and respond swiftly if an incident were to occur. This level of security was essential, as it provided a buffer against the violent tactics of insurgent groups. However, it also served as a stark reminder of the inherent risks of working in such a hostile environment.

In the eyes of the Taliban, engineers like Karan were seen as soft targets—individuals whose safety could be exploited to further their nefarious agendas. The Taliban viewed these engineers not only as valuable captives but also as symbols of the foreign presence and influence they vehemently opposed. The abduction or harm of an engineer could disrupt projects, send a powerful message, and be used as leverage in negotiations or propaganda. This made the role of security personnel even more critical, as they were the first and often the only line of defense against such threats. The constant vigilance required to protect against these dangers added an additional layer of stress and complexity to the already demanding work of engineering in a conflict zone.

***

It didn't help when his colleagues, who had been on this project longer than he had, would tell Karan about the previous cities they were based in. Lashkar Gah, Herat, Kandahar – these cities haunted their dreams and their waking moments. They spoke about the Taliban firing, the nights they had to brave with fear gnawing at their resolve. The tales of relentless violence and sleepless nights became a backdrop to their current mission, instilling a sense of foreboding in Karan's mind.

As each day turned to night at his base camp, Karan would thank the heavens that there wasn't any firing that day. His silent thanks continued until the forty-fifth day. Because the open firing began on the forty-sixth day. Karan could feel his heart sink, knowing this was probably going to be one of the toughest nights of his life. The air grew tense, and every distant noise made him flinch, anticipating the worst.

"Guess our lucky streak is over," Karan thought in dismay, as he watched the firing. It felt like a scene out of the old war movies he had seen. But to see it in real life? It was absolutely surreal!

It's odd to witness firing. It looked like fireflies had adorned the skies – only these were deadly fireflies and you had to keep your head down and stay out of the way! No one wished to get caught in the crossfire. Everyone had undergone training and drills to know what to do in case of firing. They were supposed to head to the bunker and let the soldiers do their job. The bunker went deep into the ground, designed to keep them safe. Sometimes, if the firing began without warning, there wouldn't be time to grab anything to protect against stray bullets. They would grab the bucket and a towel, run to the bunker as demonstrated, and stay there all night long.

In the morning, when the rescue team would come to get them, they would emerge to a grim scene, surrounded by those who lost their lives during the firing. It was both people from the Taliban and some of their security personnel. Even then, they had to go back to building the highway, figuring out their calculations – this danger, the constant threat looming over their heads of losing their lives, was a part and parcel of this job. Karan thought they all knew they couldn't just opt out of it. Karan and his team had to find a way to accept that this was just how their lives were now. In some weeks, they did.

The adjustment wasn't easy. Nights were filled with anxious whispers and fitful sleep, while days were spent with heightened alertness and a lingering sense of vulnerability. Despite the training and the routine, the unpredictability of their situation weighed heavily on them. But in time, Karan and his colleagues learned to compartmentalize their fear, focusing on the tasks at hand and finding solace in the camaraderie that bound them together.

***

To ensure their safety, there were two supervisors stationed on the left and right sides of the construction site, vigilantly scanning the distance to make sure the Taliban didn't suddenly pay a visit. The telltale sign of the Taliban was their use of a red Land Cruiser. However, even when such a vehicle was spotted and kept under surveillance, our lookout would sometimes witness nothing more than a family passing through in peace. The team tried to stay one step ahead, doing their best to navigate the project with as little conflict as possible. But sometimes, things just happened, and no one could do anything about it except keep oneself safe.

Another incident that became etched in Karan's memory was when they were cautioned about the landmines planted around their work area. For 38 kilometers, on both the left and right sides of the road, anti-tank mines had been laid. These mines were a parting gift from Russia during their unsuccessful invasion of northern Afghanistan. Although Russia had conceded defeat, they left behind a deadly reminder of their presence.

Karan and his co-workers had to tread carefully. Usually, their chaperones would mark a safe passage for them by following the steps of a donkey. "You could just let us borrow the donkey," Karan had once insisted, "Instead of you always hovering around us like babysitters!" They had agreed, and for a while, it worked. That is until the donkey stepped on a landmine and was blown to smithereens.

All the engineers ran back to their base camp, unable to process what they had just witnessed. The scene left them shaken, reinforcing the ever-present danger they faced daily.

Years later, Karan can laugh about the incident, but he hasn't been able to shake off the feeling of uncertainty that his time in Afghanistan gifted him. The constant vigilance, the underlying tension, and the unpredictable threats were experiences that left an indelible mark on his psyche. Every step they took, every task they performed, was shadowed by the knowledge that their lives could change in an instant. Despite the years that have passed, the memories of those perilous days remain vivid, a testament to the resilience and adaptability required to survive in such hostile environments.

***

In a war-ridden zone, where everyone is constantly trying to stay alive, there is little to nothing for entertainment. The only thing they had that came close was Buzkashi: the Afghan game of carcass and power. The objective of Buzkashi is for riders to seize control of the carcass and carry it across a goal line or into a scoring area, known as the "Circle of Justice" or "tudabarai." Riders must demonstrate exceptional riding skills, agility, and strength to maneuver the carcass amidst the chaos of the game, all while fending off competitors who seek to snatch it away. The fierce competition and the physical demands of Buzkashi provided a rare distraction from the dangers and monotony of their environment, offering moments of exhilaration and a sense of normalcy.

One particular day stands out amidst the chaos and uncertainty that defined Karan's time in Afghanistan—a day marked by a test of integrity and moral fortitude in the face of adversity. Karan's Pakistani contractor, tasked with executing crucial construction work on-site, cited a shortage of boulder stones as an excuse for the slow progress of the project. With a delegation from the World Bank due to visit the site, time was of the essence, and any delays could have serious repercussions. The pressure was immense, and the contractor's frustration was palpable, as the success of the project hinged on their ability to meet the deadlines.

In a bold and audacious move, the Pakistani contractor proposed a solution that raised eyebrows and tested the boundaries of ethical conduct. He suggested that Karan order his security personnel to fire rocket launchers at the high plateau in the valley, causing rocks to dislodge and roll down to the ground, where they could be utilized for construction purposes. The prospect of expediting the project by unconventional means was enticing, and they offered Karan a substantial sum of money in exchange for compliance. It was a moment that could have easily swayed someone less principled, especially under such dire circumstances.

"No," Karan said, firmly. He didn't care how much money was being offered. He had been raised on certain morals and principles. He wouldn't be swayed by that at all.

"Will you not even consider it?" the man had pressed on.

"No, I will not," he said firmly and walked away from the situation. He couldn't believe how people could just accept bribes and shrug their shoulders when confronted about it. He had learned the hard way that there were no shortcuts to success. He couldn't understand how other people had absolutely no problem just doing immoral things and chalking it up to life being unfair.

However, Karan remained steadfast in his refusal, unwavering in his commitment to uphold the values of honesty and integrity even in the face of adversity. Karan's actions not only garnered respect and admiration from his colleagues but also fostered a sense of trust and honesty among all the contractors involved in the project. By standing firm in his principles, he not only upheld his own integrity but also set a precedent for ethical conduct that reverberated throughout the project site. His decision became a defining moment, one that highlighted the importance of maintaining ethical standards even in the most challenging environments.

Another incident from his time in Afghanistan has taken a fond place in Karan's memory. Despite having no access to alcohol or drugs, he would regularly find himself feeling high and dizzy, with his eyes bloodshot. "We cannot be high," Karan had complained once, "How can we get all the symptoms of being high, and actually not be high?" His confusion was met with a surprising revelation.

"Because of the opium field a little way off," one of the security personnel told him, offhandedly.

"Excuse me?" Karan asked, in disbelief.

"There's an opium field a little way off. When they cut down the flowers, it mixes with the air, and that's what you've been getting high on... without your consent."

"Ohh," Karan replied, finally understanding the mysterious symptoms. The unintentional exposure to opium fumes added an unusual and surreal element to his already extraordinary experience in Afghanistan, a reminder of the unpredictable and often bizarre circumstances they had to navigate daily.

Karan was well-liked among his peers for his dedication, integrity, and relentless work ethic. As a young site engineer, he quickly earned the respect of his colleagues in Afghanistan, where he had been posted on a major construction project. The challenging environment only fueled his determination to prove himself. To those who knew him, Karan was a model of loyalty—a man who could always be counted on to do the right thing.

However, everything changed one fateful day when the company's chairman arrived at the site for an inspection. What was meant to be a routine visit, designed to assess progress and boost morale, soon had far-reaching consequences that no one could have predicted.

Karan's journey to Afghanistan had been unexpected. It all began when the chairman, an old friend of Karan's father, extended a helping hand. Remembering their school days together, the chairman offered Karan a job as a site engineer, knowing the young man was eager to make his mark. Grateful for the opportunity, Karan eagerly accepted the offer, excited to take on the challenge ahead.

On the day of the chairman's visit, the atmosphere at the site was tense. Everyone understood the importance of making a good impression. As the chairman toured the site, he eventually convened a meeting with the project head and the senior engineers. After discussing various aspects of the project, the chairman casually asked, "By the way, where is Karan? He's a friend's son, and I personally deputed him to this site."

The room fell silent. The project head froze, and the senior engineers exchanged uneasy glances. They had known Karan as a diligent worker, but this revelation changed everything. Suddenly, Karan was no longer just another engineer—he was someone with a direct line to the chairman, someone who might be watching their every move and reporting back.

The chairman's words planted seeds of doubt in the minds of the senior engineers. They began to question Karan's presence at the site. Was he there to spy on them? Was he secretly gathering information to report to the chairman? The thought that Karan could be an informant gnawed at them, and a subtle shift in behavior began to take place.

The camaraderie that had once defined their relationship gave way to suspicion and jealousy. Conversations grew more guarded, and Karan found himself increasingly isolated. Unbeknownst to him, the other engineers were quietly speculating about his role. They wondered if every problem on-site, every delay, every misstep, was being reported back to the chairman. The idea that Karan might be undermining them in secret turned their unease into resentment.

Before long, rumors began to swirl. Some whispered that Karan had been sent to keep an eye on the team, to act as the chairman's eyes and ears. Others took it further, suggesting that he was using his position to engage in illicit activities. The most damaging of these rumors accused Karan of stealing cement bags from the site and selling them in the local market. It was a baseless charge, but in the charged atmosphere, the truth mattered little. Perception had taken over, and in their minds, Karan was guilty.

Karan was blindsided by the sudden change in his colleagues' behavior. The once-friendly faces now turned cold, and the distance they kept was palpable. He had no idea what had caused this shift, and he could only speculate about what might have gone wrong. It wasn't until he overheard a conversation between two senior engineers that the truth began to dawn on him.

The chairman's offhand comment had set off a chain reaction of suspicion and mistrust. The very connection that had brought Karan to Afghanistan had become a source of his downfall. The more he tried to bridge the growing gap, the more his colleagues withdrew. Their suspicion only deepened, fed by jealousy and fear.

Karan's situation deteriorated rapidly. The accusations grew louder, and the senior engineers openly questioned his integrity. It didn't matter that Karan had done nothing wrong—he was already judged in their eyes. The accusations of theft and betrayal weighed heavily on him, tarnishing his reputation and undermining his hard-earned credibility.

In the end, Karan learned a painful lesson about the power of perception. The very qualities that had made him an asset—his loyalty, his dedication, his connection to the chairman—had become liabilities in an environment clouded by suspicion. He realized that no matter how hard one works, no matter how pure one's intentions, a single comment or misunderstanding can change everything. Trust, once broken, is nearly impossible to rebuild.

Karan's story serves as a cautionary tale about the dangers of favoritism and the corrosive effect of jealousy. It highlights how easily relationships can be poisoned by doubt, and how quickly respect can turn into resentment. Most importantly, it shows that even the most loyal and dedicated individuals can find themselves the target of baseless accusations, simply because of who they are connected to.

Then Karan made a bold decision—he chose to walk away. With dignity and resolve, he resigned from his job and returned home, determined to reclaim his sense of self-worth and rebuild his shattered dreams.

While enjoying a break with his sweet kids and family from work, he received news that spread like wildfire—his former senior engineer had met a tragic end. When the senior engineer was going on leave to India, company policy required everyone to report to the regional office in Kabul for induction and ticket arrangements. During the engineer's stay in Kabul, disaster struck. An oil-based heater in his room caught fire, forcing the engineer and his roommates to flee. They successfully exited the room, but the senior engineer made a fatal mistake. Despite his roommates' warnings about the imminent danger of the heater exploding, he re-entered the room, determined to retrieve the bundles of U.S. dollars he had hidden—money earned from bribes and the sale of cement and other construction materials, the very crimes for which Karan had been falsely accused.

The heater exploded, and the ensuing fire consumed the room. The senior engineer's body was torn apart, and the stolen money was scattered across the floor. The truth was laid bare for all to see—the man who had orchestrated Karan's downfall was, in fact, the true thief and betrayer.

The revelation was a sobering reminder of the Buddhist proverb that "three things cannot long be hidden: the sun, the moon, and the truth." Despite the veil of deception that had clouded the truth for a time, justice prevailed in the end, illuminating the darkness and exposing the lies that had threatened to tear lives apart.

Karan, with a renewed sense of purpose, understood that the truth would eventually come to light, no matter how deeply it was buried.

CHAPTER - TWO

After completing his stint in Afghanistan, Karan came back to India. However, he was in the

country exactly one month before a work opportunity in Libya, North Africa called him away.

He went there happily! For one thing, there were no security issues here. It wasn't a war-ravaged

a country like Afghanistan. There were a lot of stark differences between his previous

job and his current one.

The food, Karan found, was much better here. A bread that was made locally was something

that they came to enjoy. They also didn't have to live in constant fear for their lives. The local

people, Karan and his workers found were rather fond of Indians. They would go out of their

way to make their stay in Libya as pleasant as possible. However, it took a while for him and

his crew to realise this!

The only thing that wasn't working in their favor was the weather. It was hot all the time. They

were working in a town close to Al-ʿAzīzīyah, which has been recorded to be the hottest city in

the entire world. It holds the world record for being 58 degrees Celsius, on the 13th of September

1992. Working in this hot weather condition was next to impossible but still, Karan and his team

soldered on! This time, he wasn't one of the workers. He was the Project Manager. Their job

was installing water pipes and sewage pipes in the towns. And even though the heat was getting

to them, since they had committed to doing a job, they didn't complain and worked towards

achieving their goal.

Much like in Afghanistan, here too, the cooks in the base camp used to cook their lunches and

pack them for them. It was during one of these lunch breaks that Karan noticed something

peculiar. A woman wearing a burqa and a child came out of one of the houses set up a

dining table, and lay a *dastarkhwan* tablecloth on it. Then, they laid out a variety of food on it

— including ice cream, cold drinks, juices, and various kinds of fruits. This wasn't a one-off case.

If a street had twenty houses, all twenty of them would do the same. Not sure what to make

of these tables laden with food, Karan and his team stuck to their packed lunches. Until, one

day, a man approached them.

"Why don't you ever touch the food that's laid out for you on the dining tables? They are offered

with love."

"Oh, they never said anything. We didn't know what to make of the food." Karan replied taken

aback.

"Well, it's for you and your team. You should definitely have it," the man encouraged him.

"But...why are you doing this? I don't understand. We're just doing our jobs," Karan said, a

little flabbergasted by the attention they were getting suddenly.

"It's because you're working in this heat," the man explained, "we are quite ashamed that we

are not able to contribute to this work. But what we can do is offer you fresh food during lunch.

It's a token of our appreciation. Besides – we really like Indians. And we're grateful you're here

making our towns better with your work."

It was the locals' way of thanking them for their hard work. Karan was touched by this gesture. Once they learned that the food was meant for them things changed for everyone. Since then, onwards, no one brought packed lunches to the work site. Instead, they would enjoy themselves at the tables with the amazing spreads. It was still tedious working in the heat but the break they received during lunch, feasting on fresh food, made everything worth it. And they went back to work in the second half with renewed vigor!

***

Karan began to notice that his workers were overeating during their lunches and overpacking

food for their snacks during their journey back home. The workers were in a bus ahead of his

car. The project manager traveled in a car with a driver, behind the bus. He noticed that his

workers would sometimes throw the extra bread and fruits out of the bus window into the

streets. It filled him with embarrassment when he noticed the richer locals (who were mostly

Muslims) get down from their expensive cars like BMWs pick up that trash and get their streets

clean again!

"Guys, please eat as much as you know you'll able to eat," Karan advised the workers, "There's no reason to take more than you can eat, and then waste the remaining. Wasting food isn't a

good look on us. Especially when the local people are going out of their way to ensure we have

access to good, fresh, and healthy food."

This advice had an impact on the workers, and they stopped wasting food like they were doing

previously. They became more mindful of the food that they were consuming, and grateful that

despite the extreme weather conditions, they were able to enjoy their lunches and their snacks!

***

While Karan was happy to be working in North Africa, he had a very personal reason for wanting

to come here. You see, when he was hardly 8 or 9 years old, in the year 1982, he had challenged

his dad that he would come here!

Around the early 1980s, his father had gone to North Africa as a contractor, to help build 103

bungalows in a small town. Back then, air travel wasn't as commonplace as it is today. It was

considered very prestigious. So going to receive someone from the airport was considered a

really big deal.

"Take me with you, I want to receive Papa too," eight-year-old Karan had begged of his uncles.

"No, we're not going to take a child with us to the airport," the uncles had scoffed, dashing his

dreams of going to the airport.

Karan was upset. His anger and hurt spilled onto the next few hours when his father came back

and gifted him toys and clothes. He didn't accept those – so great was his anger at being denied

his small request!

"Areh, why are you so mad?" his father inquired, after realizing Karan wasn't happy or cheerful

about his return.

"I asked to be taken to the airport to receive you, and they refused to take me," Karan said,

sullenly. "But one day, I'll go where you had gone."

He was not even in his double digits and he had already set a goal for himself. No amount of coaxing and cajoling would get him to forgive his father. Karan was too young to understand that it wasn't his father's decision that he had been left behind. Rather, it had been the other uncles who had decided not to bring him along when they went to get *his* father from the airport. He couldn't get over the injustice of it all. And he was determined that one day he would make good on his promise and go where his father had gone before him.

Now years later, when he was in North Africa, on a Friday when he had a day off, he asked his

driver to take him to a small town called Bani Walid. Since there was no Google back then, they

had to do their research manually. All he remembered was the name of the town.

"Do you know the exact place where an Indian company built 103 bungalows in the early 1980s?"

he would keep asking at every stop, and be directed to a newer place.

Finally, they came to what promised to look like the place his father had worked in all those years ago. They rang the doorbell to one of the bungalows and one of the tenants came out.

"Excuse me, do you know when these bungalows were built?" he asked.

"I believe between 1979 and 1983," the man answered, bewildered.

But it confirmed Karan's suspicion. He knew he was at the right place, and his younger self was

as happy as a clown realizing he'd made his childhood challenge a success! He called his parents

right then to tell them about it.

"Papa, do you remember when I was eight and I wasn't taken to the airport to receive you?"

Karan asked, over the phone.

"Yes," his father said, recalling the incident.

"And do you remember how I'd told you that one day I'd be at the same place as you had been

years and years ago?" he pressed on.

"Of course," his father said, smiling at the thought. Little Karan could be extremely stubborn

when he wanted to.

"I am there right now," he said, gleefully, "I did what I said I'd do all those years ago!"

"What?!" his father, shrieked.

"I always knew you're obstinate," his mother said, suppressing her laughter, "I am glad you

used it to do good things."

He was only eight when he decided he would show them all one day by coming to the same

place as his father! It had taken years, but he had finally done it. His heart was singing with

happiness.

He didn't know it then but his single-minded determination would be the reason he survived through much more challenging situations. At that moment, he was eight years old and happily celebrating achieving a goal he had set for himself all those years ago!

***

Karan's project was going well in Libya. The weather also calmed down. Karan had become

accustomed to his new life and routine. During this time, one of his childhood friends, Prasad,

called him. Prasad had a garment business that wasn't doing too well. He needed to find a job as soon as possible, to make ends meet.

"Karan, please hire me in your company as a supervisor or a foreman, please. I need a job

desperately," he pleaded over the phone.

"Yes," Karan said, at once, "I'll see what I can do."

At once, he went to my immediate supervisor and told him about Prasad. Karan didn't mince

my words while vouching for his friend. "He doesn't have much experience, but I can guarantee

if trained well, he'll learn things quickly, and produce high-quality work."

"Alright," Karan's supervisor agreed, "Let me interview him, and we'll see what can be done."

Prasad passed his telephonic interview with flying colours. Within 20 to 25 days of that

interview, he was in Libya with his childhood friend, working on his site. Karan felt like he could

breathe easily again!

When you're living away from home, and adjusting to a life that's different from the one you're used to, even a shred of familiarity makes things easier for you. Prasad provided Karan with

the reminder and anchor he needed for home. Despite the vast differences in their posts, with Karan being a project manager, and Prasad being a mere worker, Karan insisted that they room together. Because friends are friends – no matter their positions in the office!

"I'll accommodate you in my room," Karan said, with finality, "Besides, after a long day at

work, it'll give us a chance to chit-chat during the evening."

Both Karan and Prasad fell into a comfortable routine. They would go to their respective work in the morning, and in the evening when they came back to their room, they would be chatting like friends. It gave Karan a break from missing his family constantly. It also gave Prasad a sense of belonging in this otherwise alien city.

Soon, another supervisor came on board the project. For him, it was the first time coming abroad. Once the novelty had worn off, he began to feel extremely homesick!

***

It wasn't easy applying for leave when Karan was posted in Libya. The company had to apply

for exit visas on behalf of their employees. To make matters worse, the company would keep their passports in their custody. They preferred to hire people who would stay in Libya for 2-3

years without wanting to visit their families back home in India.

In case someone had an emergency, or was required to be home for some time, the company

wouldn't help them. The people in Karan's team believed that due to the intricate process of

applying for exit visas, the company used to be quite rude about letting people go home on

leave.

While Karan knew that it was an unethical practice, there was little to nothing he could do about it. He promised himself that the moment he became a manager, he would ensure that all the people who reported to him would be granted access to go home to their families whenever an emergency presented itself.

***

"When my wife passed away ten years ago, I wanted desperately to return home," recounted one of the seasoned workers, now 62 years old, his voice tinged with sorrowful reminiscence. "I begged and pleaded with my supervisors. All I wanted was to bid her a proper farewell, to perform her last rites, but my requests for leave were denied repeatedly."

Karan, visibly taken aback by the heart-wrenching tale, inquired softly, "When did you finally manage to make the journey back home?"

The man's response was laden with bitterness, yet tinged with a resigned smile, "Would you believe it? It took nearly a year and a half. I missed being there for my wife's funeral, unable to even say goodbye properly."

Karan was stunned. He couldn't understand how could companies be this cruel to their employees. After all, weren't humans the ones who were running these companies in the first place? He hoped that he would be able to make a difference if he found someone suffering in a similar manner.

In stark contrast, a youthful 24-year-old, who had initially been thrilled to embark on his first overseas assignment with Prasad, soon found the novelty of foreign shores fading into homesickness. Within just a couple of months, his initial excitement gave way to a deep longing for home. Despite his earnest pleas to return falling on deaf ears, the weight of separation began to take a toll on him both mentally and physically. His demeanor shifted drastically; once a vibrant young man, he became withdrawn and despondent. His physical health deteriorated visibly, his face contorted with anxiety, often drooling involuntarily, and eventually, he ceased attending work altogether.

Recognizing the severity of the situation, the company's vice-president, during a routine visit, was moved by the collective concern of his colleagues.

Witnessing firsthand the young man's declining state, he swiftly intervened, personally investigating the matter. Alarmed by what he observed, he wasted no time in contacting the Director, urging immediate action. Within a matter of days, all necessary arrangements—passport, visa, and tickets—were expedited, ensuring the young man's swift repatriation.

Karan, who had seen the transformation from despair to hope in his colleague's eyes, shared in the collective relief. Over the following days, he listened as the young man excitedly planned his return—reuniting with family, revisiting cherished places, and relishing the comfort of home-cooked meals. Witnessing the profound impact of a compassionate response to human needs left an indelible impression on Karan, reaffirming the importance of empathy in the workplace amidst the challenges of expatriate life.

These contrasting narratives underscored the dichotomy of experiences among expatriate workers—a poignant reminder of the human cost behind stringent leave policies and the vital role of compassionate leadership in mitigating personal crises amid professional responsibilities.

"You're tickets back home are done," Karan told the fellow worker with a broad smile. He watched as a grin broke across his co-worker's face, transforming his usual stoic expression into one of pure joy. For the next few days, all Karan heard was what the guy planned to do when he got back home. He eagerly talked about all the places he'd visit with friends, all the things he wanted to do with his family and the specific dishes he'd ask his mother to prepare because he missed the food so much. Karan had never seen anyone this happy, and the excitement was contagious.

The workers in Libya, especially those from other countries, were always terrified of the passport withholding and exit visa policies. These rules kept them bound to their jobs, unable to leave even if they desperately wanted to. The fear of being stuck in a foreign land without the possibility of returning home haunted them daily. They didn't know what would happen if, God forbid, something happened back home and they were required to be there immediately. This fear was a constant undercurrent, affecting their well-being and peace of mind. Needless to say, those who had come to Libya purely for monetary gain were not as troubled by these restrictions and tended to stay for long periods without much fuss.

Within 18 months, Karan completed his part of the project and returned home. He continued to travel all over the world for both business and pleasure, savoring the freedom and experiences each journey brought. On the other hand, Prasad, his colleague, decided to stay back and continue with the job in Libya. Prasad's decision was driven by different priorities and circumstances, illustrating the diverse reasons people choose to stay or leave their jobs in challenging environments.

Karan would miss not rooming with a friend. He would miss not having someone to share his homesickness with. But he also knew that people chose different things according to their needs and desires. He bid farewell to Prasad and wished him well.

"What's next for you?" Prasad asked him, as he saw off his friend.

"Go home for a bit," Karan said, honestly, "Rest and then see what is out there for me. In our line of work, we seem to be able to go all around the world in the blink of an eye."

"And put ourselves in danger all the time too," Prasad said, laughing.

"Well, no risk, no reward," Karan said, smiling at his friend.

Over the years, they would keep in touch. Friendship, after all, is a bond that survives through the toughest of situations. It is one of the strongest bonds you can have in the world!

***

Around three to four years later, when Karan was in Singapore, he was watching the news one day. His heart sank as he saw the horrifying news that the President of Libya had been assassinated by the local public. A civil war had erupted, plunging the country into chaos. There was open firing everywhere, and it was just utter pandemonium. Horrified, Karan immediately called Prasad to inquire about his safety and well-being.

"We're not safe," Prasad said sadly over the phone. "Our basecamp has been infiltrated. The army is here, trying to contain the matter, but it's getting out of hand. There are six of us here hiding out in our Libya translator's house."

The situation was dire. Airports were closed, shutting down all hopes of an escape for most people. The streets were scenes of violent unrest, with people throwing rocks and setting things on fire. It was an impossible situation to escape from. Somehow, things managed to get even worse. The locals had begun robbing the expatriates. If they found non-Libyans, they would either kill them or loot them. Fear gripped everyone, making the already dire circumstances even more unbearable.

Due to the rising unrest in the city, their translator decided to drive them to another city where his relatives were waiting. But as luck would have it, their car was stopped only after 20-25 kilometers. All their phones and cash were stolen, leaving them stranded and helpless.

Three days later, Karan finally got a call from an unknown number. It was Prasad. "We've reached a town near the sea," he explained. "They put us on a ship, and we came via the sea to this new town. We're safe for now. The Indian Government is trying its best to evacuate us from Libya currently. But the situation is just so terrible right now. There's firing going on every single night! If we peep outside, we can see dead bodies lying all around. And every single man is looting every single house. It's utter madness here!"

Karan continued to follow the news, feeling utterly helpless. The Indian Government had sent special aircraft to Libya to help evacuate people, but it was a slow and uncertain process. All he could do was follow the news, wonder what was happening, and pray for good news from his friend. The waiting was agonizing, filled with worry and a deep sense of impotence.

Finally, he got a call from a Tunisian number. Tunisia is a neighboring country of Libya. It was Prasad calling him. "We're in the custody of the Ministry of External Affairs and the Tunisian Army," Prasad said. "They allowed me to make a phone call. I'm calling to let you know I'm safe. But this place is overcrowded with people wanting to go home. We have a draw system, and we need to wait our turn to go back."

Tunisia was ill-prepared to take care of the expatriates. They had no room to accommodate them, no arrangements for food, clean bathrooms, or even drinking water. They had escaped one disaster only to end up in another dire situation. No one knew when they would get to go home. Everyone had to wait for their passport number to be called, and it seemed like fate would decide if and when they got to return home.

This was when both Karan and Prasad remembered that Prasad's cousin, Mr. Vikrant, worked in the Ministry of External Affairs. He was posted in Norway at that time. So, Karan decided to call him. "Mr. Vikrant, are you aware that your cousin is currently in Tunisia, waiting to come home?" Karan asked. "Could you make a phone call and see if arrangements can be made for him to come back home safely?"

Vikrant, understanding the gravity of the situation, made the necessary calls immediately and pulled some strings. Within no time, travel arrangements were made for Prasad and four more people. However, the sixth person in their group began crying. He begged them not to leave him behind, fearing he wouldn't be able to make it on his own.

"Don't worry," Prasad assured the weeping gentleman. "We'll go together." He asked the authorities to call them when they had six seats available instead. Within a few hours, they got the six seats they required and were on their way to India. When they landed, they were greeted by medical care, food, water, and other necessary arrangements provided by the airport authorities and the government.

After being unsure for so long if they'd even get to come back home, fearing for their lives constantly, it was a profound relief to finally be back again. All around, it was a happy reunion. Families were tearfully embracing their loved ones, and there was a collective sense of gratitude and relief.

Grateful to have had his friend by his side through this ordeal, Prasad placed a call to Karan, who answered on the very first ring.

"I am back home," Prasad wept, "It has been one of the most challenging times of my life. But I am home and safe. And it's all thanks to you."

"I am just glad I was able to get the help you needed to come back home," Karan said, smiling in relief that his friend was safe and sound. "Welcome home, Prasad."

"We should catch up soon, Karan," Prasad joked, "Let me know when you're back in town as well."

This harrowing experience underscored the importance of having robust systems in place for the protection and evacuation of expatriates during times of crisis. It also highlighted the need for international cooperation and the invaluable role of diplomatic channels in ensuring the safety of citizens abroad. Karan and Prasad's ordeal serves as a powerful reminder of the vulnerabilities faced by workers in foreign lands and the urgent need for policies that safeguard their rights and well-being.

In the end, the ordeal brought Karan and Prasad closer, deepening their bond forged in the fires of adversity. They both carried the scars of their experience but also the knowledge that they had survived a nightmare, thanks to their resilience and the timely intervention of those who cared. This story, with all its twists and turns, is a testament to the enduring human spirit and the unbreakable ties of friendship and family.

CHAPTER - THREE

After Karan came back from Libya, he spent around 45 days in India with his family. During this

time, he took his family to Bikaner to worship Karni Mata. The Karni Mata Temple in Deshnok,

Bikaner is a revered Hindu temple dedicated to Karni Mata, a Hindu goddess considered to be

an incarnation of Durga. This temple is renowned for its unique inhabitants: thousands of rats,

regarded as sacred and worshipped by devotees.

Visitors to the Karni Mata Temple are astounded by the sight of these rats freely roaming around

the premises, fed and cared for by the temple priests and devotees. It is considered fortunate

to spot a white rat among the swarm, as it is believed to be a manifestation of Karni Mata

herself Overall, it proved to be a good vacation.

When they came back home from the trip, Karan interviewed for a job in Dubai. He got selected as a Project Manager for a mega project. It was going to be a huge responsibility. He would have to oversee the mega project! There was immense pressure to deliver this project on time. The company showed immense faith in his capabilities and was sure he would deliver the project within the discussed timeline. The prestigious car racing trophy was going to be held there – hence the insane deadline for the project! Now, while Karan gave his project his all, getting involved in all its nitty-gritty, the upper management didn't seem to trust that he would be able to pull off the project. Or at least, that's what Karan would feel from their vibes. Maybe they didn't have as much faith in his abilities as the hiring manager!

Karan walked through the construction site with a sense of unease. The scene before him was all too familiar, reminiscent of what he had witnessed in Libya and Dubai. In Libya, workers had thoughtlessly discarded food given to them by locals, showing no regard for the generosity or the waste they were creating. In Dubai, the situation was similar—workers left their leftovers near the garbage area instead of placing them inside bins. This carelessness led to piles of food rotting in the heat, attracting pests and spreading foul odors.

Now, here at this site, history was repeating itself. Over a thousand workers from India were stationed here, and many had adopted the same careless habits. Food was tossed outside, where it accumulated and began to decompose, emitting a stench that hung in the air like a heavy fog. Flies and other insects swarmed the area, making the site increasingly unhygienic.

Karan couldn't help but recall the proverb: "Waste not, want not." The workers' actions had created a serious problem, one that threatened the health and safety of everyone on-site. The site's Health & Safety Officer confirmed Karan's fears during an inspection, warning the Admin Officer that the garbage had to be removed immediately to prevent disease.

The Admin Officer instructed his team to clear the garbage, but when Karan returned the next day, nothing had changed. Furious, Karan called the Admin Officer to his office, demanding an explanation. The Admin Officer admitted that he had tried to clear the garbage, but the supervisors refused, claiming it wasn't their duty. Some even said they would rather be terminated and sent back to India than clean the mess.

Karan was caught in a dilemma. He knew the garbage had to be removed immediately to avoid severe consequences. That night, an idea struck him. It was bold and unconventional, but it might just work.

The next morning, Karan called out to the Admin Officer, "Bring me a shovel. You and I will clean this mess ourselves." Without waiting for a response, Karan grabbed the shovel and began to clean the garbage. The workers watched in stunned silence as their leader got his hands dirty without hesitation.

As Karan worked, he recalled the words of Mahatma Gandhi: "The best way to find yourself is to lose yourself in the service of others." His actions weren't just about cleaning up the garbage; they were about setting an example.

Minutes later, workers joined Karan, ashamed of their carelessness. Soon, more workers followed, and within a short time, the entire site was spotless. The workers felt a deep sense of guilt and responsibility, approaching Karan to apologize for their behavior.

"We're sorry, sir," one worker said. "From now on, we'll never throw food outside the garbage area."

Karan nodded, his voice calm but firm. "Thank you for your effort. Remember, it's not just about disposing of food properly. Eat only what you need. Wasting food is never a good idea. Let's be grateful that we have enough to eat, three times a day. Count your blessings."

The workers understood the deeper message behind Karan's words. It wasn't just about cleanliness; it was about respect—for their work, each other, and the resources they were fortunate to have. Karan's actions had turned a potential disaster into a powerful lesson in unity and responsibility.

That day, the workers learned that true leadership isn't about issuing orders but leading by example. As the proverb goes, "Actions speak louder than words." Karan's actions had spoken volumes, and the workers would carry that lesson with them long after the site was cleared.

However, the upper management had a relative named Mr. Parekh. He was the head of the Gulf

Countries. For whatever reason, he understood Karan and trusted him completely. He trusted

Karan completely and under his guidance, the Dubai project was successfully completed.

However, during this time, the world was hit by the global recession. All the projects in Dubai

came to a stop. Since Mr. Parekh knew of Karan's calibre, his hardships, and his honesty, so he

offered Karan work elsewhere. At this point in time, Mr. Parekh had projects in the Commonwealth

Independence States (CIS) countries. This used to be in the USSR. The project would be

somewhere in Turkmenistan. The head of the company there had left his job.

"I am extremely impressed with the work you've done here, Karan," Mr. Parekh told him,

"Would you be interested in going to Turkmenistan? It won't be your old role. You'll be going

as the Country Head and oversee projects there."

"Of course, Sir," Karan replied, delighted. He had been worrying about what he was going to

do now that the Dubai projects were halted.

Probing further, Karan discovered that it wasn't one or two projects – but numerous projects –

for ministries, for governments, etc. these were all going to be major projects. So, he packed

his things and left for Turkmenistan.

45

CHAPTER - FOUR

Here, Karan discovered that Russian culture is different from other cultures. The working

experience in Dubai had been completely different. It's widely believed that the work culture

in Dubai is the toughest. And if they can survive working in Dubai, they are held in high esteem.

The weather conditions were extreme, and so were the working conditions. Workers were expected

to wake up at 4 am and come back from the site at 8 pm. There was hardly any time to eat

dinner and go to bed – rinse and repeat. Due to this, in the construction field, it was believed

that anyone who experienced, survived, and thrived working in Dubai and other Gulf Countries,

was revered as a good worker. In fact, people say that if someone can work in these countries,

they can work anywhere in the world.

In stark contrast to the work culture in Dubai, was the culture in Turkmenistan – where Karan

had gone to work in the USSR. The first thing that he noted was different was his role. Even

though he had been told beforehand, that it was an adjustment to be the Country Head in the

project. There were thousands of people reporting to him – such as the project managers,

general managers, and the HRs!

But despite the pressure, the weather conditions were good. The food and drinks were amazing.

There was a bit of a language barrier though, since people here spoke Russian, rather than

English. Under compulsion, Karan learned Russian – which was the local language – to

communicate better. He got so good that in two months he was speaking it quite fluently.

Because of his new role, Karan didn't have to go to project sites. Instead, he had to go into the

office. He had meetings with the top officials of the countries. It was a lot of work and a lot of

responsibility too. But Karan was happy. To him, it felt like he had finally arrived in life.

In Turkmenistan, the culture was very vodka-centric. There was always a variety of vodkas available. And the best part? There used to be snow all around, and they would experience

snowfall, making it very pleasant work conditions to be in.

Karan believed with all his heart that life was finally fulfilled. He was overjoyed – his salary

was really good and he was holding a position at the top. He had a car, a house, a servant,

separate drivers for day and night time. He finally had everything that he had ever dreamed of. Gone were the days when we barely scraped by working at a dead-end job. That first offer to go work in Afghanistan had literally changed his life. Since then, he has been part of a lot of projects. But until right now, he had never really felt that he had really made it life. The moment he did, he needed to share the news with someone. And who else would understand what he was feeling better than his life partner? So, in his happiness, he called his wife.

"Life is amazing," he told her, happily, "We don't have to worry anymore. Everything we have

been working towards – we finally have it!"

His wife was delighted too. She merely laughed at the statement. They had years together ahead of them, they believed. He would go back and they could start taking trips together. He could finally have his family over. So many plans began to form in Karan's excited head. All the plans he had put on hold saying he would do it later or once he had enough money – it started coming home to him. He wanted to put those plans into action as soon as possible. He wanted to be with his family – his wife, and his kids. He was on cloud nine it seemed. But he had spoken too soon.

Looking back, Karan believes he shouldn't have thought or said something so arrogant. No one

would believe he had started from zero and reached the apex, and then he made such a statement that probably pissed off the Gods? Because everything came crashing down for him hardly a week later.

Karan received a call from his family that changed everything for him.

"*Beta*, your wife passed away from a sudden heart attack," they told him, "You need to come

home immediately."

In media, whenever someone receives bad news, they show that the character dissociates completely from reality. They are unable to hear anything besides a high-pitched ringing in their ears. That's exactly what Karan went through. He couldn't hear the rest of the sentence. He didn't even know if he had exchanged goodbyes. For him, time just stood still. He didn't know what to do. He seemed to be going through the motions rather than processing what he had just heard. His body and mind seemed to have gone into autopilot.

It took time for the news to sink in for him. Only seven days ago, he and his wife were happy.

They were rejoicing in their victory. What was he hearing? Was this someone's idea of a cruel

joke? He thought of his kids. They were so young during this time. His daughter was 3 years old,

and his son was 7 years old.

He had been having his dinner when he got the news. He didn't even finish the food. He froze

for what seemed like 10 minutes...15 minutes...1 hour...and even then, his mind couldn't

fathom what he had heard. He didn't even cry. He was merely existing.

"Come meet me in the office as soon as you can," Karan told the HR Head when he called him.

He knew he had to get his tickets sorted and go home. only HR would be able to help him

sort this out.

When the HR Head came around 10 pm, Karan recited what he had been told on the call. Seeing

the HR Head's reaction, the reality finally hit him – his wife was no more. He was never going

to hear her voice again, he was never going to see her smile, she would not be there to talk to

him...she was just gone.

Then he thought of all the memories his children got robbed of. His wife got robbed. She would never get to enjoy the wealth he'd managed to create for them.

She wouldn't get to see her children grow up, graduate, find their own life partners, and choose careers that brought them both joy. They wouldn't have both their parents at every important landmark of their lives. Everything seemed utterly unfair to him. And the reality that she was just gone, and there was nothing that could change hit him like a ton of bricks.

Karan broke down crying. He didn't remember how long he cried. He vaguely noticed his office staff – 20 to 30 people – had gathered around there. He didn't know how they found out what was going on. Maybe they heard his cries, maybe the HR head told them what was going on. All his workers were there with him, while he tried to process his heartbreaking news. None of them were saying nothing. Because what do you say to someone who's just received devasting news? Time heals everything is a phrase that sounds comforting in theory. In practice, some wounds might heal but the scars remain forever. But their presence was comforting to Karan – even if for a moment, he didn't feel completely alone.

Mr. Alex, the translator, was sympathetic towards Karan's situation but wasn't able to procure

tickets for him immediately. "The problem is due to snowfall. There are no tickets available.

You won't be able to leave immediately."

But that didn't mean the company didn't try its best to get Karan homeward-bound as soon as possible. They left one stone unturned to ensure that Karan could go home, be there for his two small children, and perform the last rites for his wife. The company sent people to the airlines directly to try and get tickets. Everyone stayed up all night, keeping a silent vigil for Karan's plight. Mr. Alex came back with the tickets to India. Unfortunately, though, there was a slight catch. They weren't able to get tickets that would get Karan to Delhi as quickly as possible. There were no tickets that would take him directly to Delhi. This journey had become complicated even before it started. It was going to be long-winded and tedious. And delay wasn't something Karan could afford at the time.

"We could manage to get tickets for you from Turkmenistan to Dubai, and then from there to

Jaipur. After this, you'll have to travel by car."

Karan didn't even stay around to argue. He knew time was precious. He knew right now in the current situation beggars couldn't be choosers. He had to make the best of a terrible situation. With only the thoughts of his kids in his mind, Karan set off on his journey immediately. He finally reached home. Three days after he had initially received the news of his wife's passing.

***

Karan's home in Delhi felt oddly familiar. There were people bustling around the house. He wasn't used to so many people being there. He noticed that there were around 400 – 500 people who had come down to offer their condolences and their help. They all assured him that they would all be there to help him with everything.

Karan merely nodded at their kind words and their promises. He was already feeling overwhelmed – first from the journey, and second from having the face the reality of it all – all over again. His children were too young to understand the finality of someone leaving this world forever. He shadowed him everywhere. Karan knew he had to be stronger for their sake. Even if he felt the world was going to fall apart for him, he had to be strong. He had become the sole parent for both of his kids overnight. He didn't know how he would manage to juggle being both a mom and a dad to his two kids – but he knew he didn't have another choice. So many other questions plagued him. About the mundane, the day-to-day – things his wife had usually handled. Things he probably never thought about because his wife had been the one to ensure those were done.

His children, of course, would need to get used to this new dynamic. He tried not to think about it much. He knew he was their only source of comfort and joy at the moment. He had to be strong for them. Because they were clinging to him tightly, afraid to let go. Afraid he too would disappear like their mother if they loosened their grip over him at all.

The day after Karan reached home, the family performed his wife's last rites. They went to the

*crematorium ghat**.

By the time everything was over and they came back home, it was around

2 pm – 3 pm in the afternoon. Despite his numbness, Karan noted that there were about 50

people still there with him. Everyone else had started their cars and left.

Of those 50-odd people, around 30 to 20 assured him they were going to be there with him and for him. In Karan's family, the rites for the women last for 11 days. Overnight, Karan noticed that the 50 people thinned to 20. These last 20 people were those who were very close to him – such as his maternal aunts, his paternal aunts, his in-laws, and his closest friends. They stayed the night with him.

But the people never stopped thinning. When he woke up around 10 am the very next day, he

noticed that only 8 people i.e. the family members were the only ones left now. Everyone else

had to go back to their lives. Only his life felt stuck, only his life seemed to have hit a pause,

without ever knowing when he would hit the play button again.

Crematorium Ghat: *A designated area, often along a riverbank, where Hindu funeral rites are performed, and the deceased are cremated*

He wondered about the 500-odd people he had first seen, who had dropped everything to be there with him in his time of need. But as the days went on, everyone returned to the lives that they already had. Karan didn't know how to move forward. He felt stuck. He also grimly observed how time was the thief of all joy and sadness. Just because he didn't know what to do next, didn't mean the people who had made him promises to be with him through thick and thin would be right with him. They felt sorry for him, and they no doubt felt terrible about the ordeal he was currently facing. But there wasn't much they could do for him. This was Karan's battle and Karan's alone. Even if people wanted to be there – they really couldn't. They had to return to the lives that had been interrupted by the tragedy that had befallen Karan.

Even in the haze, Karan noticed his biological brothers resumed work. His *bhabi* started with the household chores. Everyone else seemed to have gotten over their grief. The only people left grieving were just him, his children, his parents, and his father-in-law and mother-in-law.

Because for them the pain didn't stop once the rituals were over. They had to return to a life where his wife was gone, and there was nothing they could do to fill that void. There was nothing anyone could do to figure out how to fill that gap left by her death. They had to adjust to a world where she no longer existed. To Karan, that was the biggest tragedy of it all.

***

All the friends and family who had left came back on the 11th day for the final ritual. But during

the night, it was back to the core 8 family members. Karan's kids were sitting in his lap, and as

they hugged their father with their tiny limbs, Karan began to realize everyone was moving on and starting their lives. They were all getting left behind.

Around 2-3 days later, Karan's mother-in-law came and requested, "Send the kids to school.

They are falling behind in their classes."

"Yes, beta," his mother chimed in, "There's nothing they can do staying home and being sad."

In his head, he counted that this was the 16th day since the tragedy. His children were now going

back to their studies too. He seemed to be all alone in his grief now. Everyone else was back

at work, everyone was going on with their lives as if nothing had happened. That his wife's

existence had just been a blip in the universe. He'd never felt so hopelessly alone.

And then Karan learned the greatest and cruelest lesson that life has to teach – it is meant to

be lived alone. People will come and go. They will appreciate you, make fun of you, make rude

comments about you, promise to be there for you – and fail to keep that promise. Because at

the end of the day, you are alone in life. But just as this truth came home to Karan, he ended

up being pushed into the arms of depression! Each day became a battle against the relentless tide of despair, as he struggled to find solace in a world that seemed determined to abandon

him to his solitary anguish.

Perhaps his children were too young to realise the permanence of their mother's death. Or they simply couldn't stand being sad anymore. They wanted to get back to their lives. Their studies and school gave them the distraction they needed to be away from everything for a while. He had never wanted his kids to suffer. But to be the only one left who was deeply grieving his wife, really hurt Karan. The more he thought about the would have, could have, and should have – the more these thoughts spiraled out of his control.

Depression manifested in Karan's life, at first in little, and then in big ways. He had never gone a

day without shaving since he was twenty-one years old. This is because he was quite hairy. If

he didn't do something about his beard and moustache, it would grow a lot within the 8-10

hours! He really couldn't go 24 hours without shaving! But since his wife's passing, Karan didn't

want to shave his beard – much less take a shower – or take care of himself. He wondered what

the point of it all was anyway. He was beginning to lose hope. He was beginning to see the point of being alive if life couldn't even let him enjoy growing old with his partner.

During this time, his mother-in-law became a huge source of comfort and solace for him. After

all, she had lost her only child. To her, the grandchildren, and Karan were the only people left

with the slightest connection to her daughter. Karan's mother-in-law would come visit him

every other day, growing to think of him more as her son, than a son-in-law. Later on, Karan would come to understand that it was because of her intervention that he was finally able to pull himself together and start the journey of life once again.

His mother-in-law observed that he was severely depressed. Finally, after 7 to 10 days, she cleared her throat and said, "You need to shave your beard. You're beginning to look really awful!" Even though no part of him wanted to do that, he obliged. He kept her request and finally shaved. Karan knew it was a dark time. He didn't even try to get a job because to him the world seemed bleak and working seemed absolutely pointless if he couldn't share his happiness with his wife.

In the wake of his personal turmoil, Karan's mother-in-law stepped forward to assume custody

of his children, offering a beacon of hope amidst the darkness. As he witnessed her unwavering

commitment to nurturing his motherless children, Karan came to a profound understanding. He

realized that only those who had traversed the path of maternal loss themselves, like Nani* or

Massi** possessed the depth of empathy and understanding necessary to care for a child in such

circumstances.

***Nani:** A Hindi word for maternal grandmother,* ****Masee:** A colloquial Hindi term referring to a maternal aunt (mother's sister)*

In contrast, other relatives, though well-meaning, lacked an intimate connection to the pain

of motherlessness, rendering them unable to shoulder the weight of responsibility with the

the same level of compassion and insight. Through this experience, Karan gleaned the invaluable -

a lesson that genuine caregiving transcends mere familial ties, rooted instead in empathy,

understanding, and an unwavering commitment to love and nurture.

CHAPTER - FIVE

Karan continued to barely exist. About 3-4 months later, he had an infection in his stomach. When

he visited the family doctor he was advised to get an ultrasound. He understood that there was something severely wrong with him. After getting the results, he advised me to go to a hospital with more facilities that would help take care of me. A doctor friend of Karan's helped him go to the new hospital and asked him to meet with the gastroenterologist. He also asked that Karan make the specialist speak with him once.

"You need to get yourself treated soon," the specialist told him, after running a battery of tests,

"You have to get admitted to the hospital within a day."

"I wasn't prepared for this," Karan managed to choke, "I thought this was a run-of-the-mill checkup?"

Karan had gone believing this would be a routine checkup. It turned out to be anything but that. He had no idea that the condition had become so serious!

***

Over the next few days, the doctors planned Karan's surgery.

"Is this going to be a complicated surgery or a normal one?" he asked, apprehensively, as he stayed confined to the hospital bed.

"Normal one," they reassured him, "We'll discharge you in 2-3 days."

But even with their reassurances, Karan felt a dreadful sense of foreboding. He had been admitted to a renowned hospital in Delhi. The surgery would be performed by the head of the department who was a rather well-known figure. He has performed 48,000 surgeries to date. Karan was feeling quite confident that he was in good hands. He sincerely believed that his surgery would be successful and he would be as good as new. He had not given any thought to

his career or how he would provide for his children, in the wake of his wife's passing. Now there was one more bump in the road before he could get back to life again. Believing that this was just a minor setback, Karan braced himself for his surgery.

But sometimes it's all just wishful thinking!

In the blink of an eye, the forms were filled, Karan was put under anesthesia, and taken for surgery. When he woke up after the surgery, he felt really restless. He could feel a lot of pain in his stomach. He gained consciousness with a room full of doctors, and with his mother-in-law present. But he couldn't shake off the feeling that he wasn't okay. He could see the expression on everyone's faces. Even in his drowsy state, he could tell that the doctors looked nervous and his mother-in-law looked worried. He opened his mouth to speak.

However, before he could say anything, Karan started vomiting blood!

Instantly, he was rushed back to the OT – not to perform further surgeries – but to observe and see what had gone wrong the first time! When they brought him back, he had a world of questions for them. The doctors weren't really forthcoming with their answers. Karan still pressed on.

"What happened? Why am I in so much pain? Why am I vomiting blood? Why do I feel so awful?" he asked, horrified by the turn his operation had taken.

"Your surgery has failed," the nurse informed him, rather grimly. "The doctors are trying to find a substitute. They are trying to figure out how to reverse everything. They are looking for a solution. The entire doctors' team is involved in this."

The doctors were working around the clock to figure out how to make him feel better again. But even their best efforts couldn't stop the pain that he was currently in. Karan continued to vomit blood, crying, screaming, and wondering what was going on with his treatment! Absolutely no one was able to treat Karan successfully. He feared that the end had come. He didn't want this to be the way his existence came to an end.

Karan could barely recognize himself after the surgery. Things were so different for him – there was a urine bag attached to him and staples on his stomach!

***

3 days later.

Since his lungs were infected Karan started suffering from shortness of breath. His body started getting colder. His health was failing, and there were still no answers that could cure him.

But while Karan's suffering continued, his mother-in-law, Maata ji's anger with the doctors began to grow. She started screaming at them about Karan's deteriorating health.

"I brought a healthy man to this hospital," she yelled, "And he's gotten worse since you started treating him. You're ruining his health!"

The doctors tried to reassure her that Karan would be alright. But the hesitation in their voice was obvious. They had no idea what was going on with their patient. Maata ji grew worried for her grandchildren. She didn't want them to end up losing both their parents within months of each other! It would end up being a blow the children would not be able to recover from. But her yelling couldn't make the doctors magically come up with the solution to cure her son-in-law. Her anxiety manifested as anger, and the doctors themselves grew worried about the health of their patients. They knew they could not just leave Karan's health to fate. They would have to do something…anything about it. Only, no one had any idea what they could do in the first place!

Lying helplessly in his hospital bed, Karan felt that he was about to die. He didn't have any motivation to get well. And even as he lay dying, the doctors couldn't figure out what was wrong with him. From Karan's point of view, they either didn't know what was wrong or they knew and didn't wish to disclose it to him. He wondered how long he would be here, chained to this hospital bed, completely in limbo.

4-5 days later.

As if things weren't already bad enough, Karan's health took a turn for the worse. His lungs were filled with fluids. Now, he couldn't breathe at all. The doctors had to get a pulmonologist – who put in pipes and pumps through Karan's mouth – and temporarily got rid of the fluids.

As a temporary fix, Karan was also put on a course of antibiotics – Candula – and drips were attached to him – one at his feet, one at his hand. An oxygen equipment was put over his face as well. Even though the pressure was too hard, it had all been done to ensure his lungs wouldn't collapse.

Karan lay in bed as the doctors prodded and poked, and hoped that his health wouldn't get more worse than it already was. As for Karan himself, he was growing tired of his situation. He didn't even have the ability to voice his concerns about what he was currently going through.

6-7 days later.

Things weren't looking up at all. The doctors realized that they needed to act quickly or Karan wouldn't survive. The doctors said they needed to perform surgery. They took him away again, and he was told that he would come back to his senses on the 9th or 10th day. He could breathe easier now. During this time, a big pipe was inserted into his windpipe, and it reached his stomach. There were now way too many things attached to Karan's body – a urine bag, the drips on his feet and hand, the pipes! To Karan, it felt as though every part of his body had been stabbed and poked at. There wasn't much he could do in his state, except accept his fate. But if he could just get better, and go home, he would be a happy man.

***

For a really short period, Karan believed he was healing. But then...the fluids came back! He tried explaining to the doctor that whenever he was lying down flat, the fluids were going to his head, his nostrils, and his windpipe! It was causing breathing problems and he had to sit up. Because he knew all too well that the moment he lay down, everything would be blocked by the fluids.

He couldn't sleep. He couldn't sit up, because if he did that, the fluids would come to his nose! He tried again and again to explain his dilemma to the doctor! They were giving him medicines and anesthesia. He wanted to resist taking them as he was already quite addicted to medicines. To top that off, he was feeling sleepy…yet he couldn't sleep. Because he knew the minute he would sleep, he would die for the fluid would rush to his head!

For almost two whole days, Karan tried to explain the problem to the doctor.

"I am feeling sleepy. I want to sleep. Give me some medicines. I can't sit up either. Because sitting constantly is taking a toll on me too!"

To him, it felt as though he was making complete sense. But having pipes stuck down your throat will hamper your ability to coherent speech. So, despite his best efforts the doctors couldn't understand what he was trying to tell them. The situation had turned extremely dire.

***

Karan wasted away in the hospital bed on the 5th floor, where had been admitted. He kept staring at the glass wall as he spent time in agony. He was thoroughly disturbed by his condition. He couldn't sleep, he couldn't be awake, he was in a world of pain, and no one understood what he was trying to say! He felt helpless and defeated.

It was around 2 am in the morning. Everyone was fast asleep. Karan noticed that there was a chair near his bed. It was almost impossible for him to get up and reach that chair. Something had possessed him though. He believed that he could end his suffering in one swift movement. He didn't think of the future. He didn't think beyond the thought of wanting to stop the pain once and for all. He just didn't care about the future anymore. He had come to the hospital for a routine checkup, and now he couldn't even stand without someone else's help. It angered him.

With colossal effort, he got up silently, and he acted on the intrusive thought that had taken root in his head. That he'll hit the chair on the glass – it would shatter the glass. And from there he could leap into the sweet arms of eternal sleep! He would be united with his wife. It wasn't the old age plan he had always dreamed of – but it was a start, right? At least this way, he could stop suffering and he would see her again. He remembered how happy she had been the last time he had spoken to her. When he finally felt happy about being in a good place in life.

"We can finally enjoy life," he had said.

"Yes," she had laughed.

That laughter rang in Karan's ears. Wasn't it a good thing what he was doing then? He could be with her again – make up for all their lost time together. He had always told himself there would be enough time in the world to take trips with her, take the kids places, and go places together as a family – and yet, here he was. Alone, chained to a hospital bed, with no hope of getting better any time soon. Yes, this plan that had formed in his head, this plan made perfect sense to him. All he had to do was break the glass window with the chair, and the rest would be easy.

It is said that suicide is for the weak. At that moment, however, Karan realized that this task wasn't easy. Sometimes humans face certain circumstances that lead them to believe that this is their only option. Because right now, he couldn't bear it anymore. He just wanted his suffering to end. And if the doctors wouldn't do it – he wanted to take matters into his own hands. He was so focused on his momentary suffering, he completely forgot to think about the future.

Looking back now, Karan knows it was perhaps one of the lowest moments in his life. He just was unable to bear the pain any longer. But just as he picked up the chair and was about to smash the glass, his children's faces burst into his mind clear as day. In his moment of weakness, he had completely forgotten that they had just lost their mother. How could he go through with this reckless plan of his? He couldn't bear the thought of his children becoming orphans. They were both at home, expecting their father to make a full recovery, and return. How could he contribute to the cruelty they had already been exposed to by losing one parent so young? Who would look after them? Who would care for them? And even if relatives were kind enough to look after the kids – who would ensure all their heart's desires were fulfilled? Who would the kids go to when they needed to ask for favors or even permission?

If he went through with this, what would happen to his young kids? And that one thought changed everything for him! He stopped his reckless plan. It didn't solve his actual problem – he was still suffering. And no one knew what to do with him! But in that darkest hour, he chose to live, he chose to fight for another day. His children deserved to have a parent. They didn't deserve to grow up deprived of everything in this world. They were innocent creatures. They needed to have their father with them. He relaxed his breathing and went back to bed. He couldn't give up. Not yet, anyway.

***

From his 5th-floor hospital room window, Karan could see a temple in the distance. It was dedicated to Hanuman ji*. Like clockwork every day at 4 am, aarti would be performed for him. That day when it started, Karan started reading the Hanuman Chalisa**…a habit that he's kept to date. As the aarti# began that day, Karan looked over at the temple and prayed silently.

He prayed to Hanuman ji saying, "I don't know what's happening to me. I am not living, I cannot die, I can't sleep, I can't be awake, and even after telling the doctors what's going on – no one seems to understand what's going on with me."

* Hanuman Ji" A Hindu deity known for his strength, devotion, and loyalty to Lord Rama. **Hanuman Chalisa: A 40-verse hymn praising Hanuman Ji, recited for protection and courage. #Aarti: A Hindu ritual of worship involving the waving of a lamp before deities, accompanied by devotional songs.

He was feeling drowsy from the medicines so he told Hanuman ji, "I am going to sleep. There is a part of me that knows that I might now wake up once I go to sleep, because the fluids will take over my body, and my breathing might stop. However, whatever happens, we'll see. Just know that this isn't an act of suicide. I know I have a lot of life still left to live, and now I place it at your feet. You do whatever you think is best for me."

Karan went to sleep putting his fate into the hands of Hanuman ji. He didn't know if his prayer would be answered or not. All he knew was, he had faith. He recited the Hanuman Chalisa and fell asleep.

***

For 18 to 20 hours, Karan slept, without a care in the world. When he woke up, it felt like all the fluid was gone, and he was breathing normally.

It was a miracle!

That's when Karan realized that there might be a god. He also remembered that wise people say that suicide is a permanent solution to a temporary problem. He realized the mistake he had been about to make.

Now, while Karan was breathing normally, his fever shot up to 105°F! This was around the 12th or 13th day. Later, the nurses told him his condition had worsened during the time he had been sleeping. So, after work, the nurses who were from Hindu and Christian faiths, went to their respective temples and churches to pray for his recovery. They had lit candles and offered prayers, as Karan was quite young, and his kids were really small too. They shouldn't have to suffer the injustice of losing both parents! Karan became really happy hearing that.

His temperature increased again, and the stomach aches came back, with the shortness of breath. Karan found out later that he was on the ventilator for 3 whole days. They performed one more surgery on him.

It was the 17th day since he had come to the hospital. He hadn't drunk a single drop of water, and he had not consumed any food at all. It is said that people don't survive once they're put on the ventilator – but here he was – back from the ventilator and the doctors thought he would be okay again. But they still couldn't control his fever. In those 17-18 days in the hospital, his weight was reduced by 15-20 kilos.

***

Financially too, Karan wasn't doing too well. He ended up spending a substantial amount of money on his hospital expenses. That was a huge amount for him. He wasn't getting cured there either. His mother-in-law asked, "When are you planning on discharging Karan?"

"Madam, we can't do anything right now. His condition is so bad, he cannot be discharged," the doctors told her.

But the determined lady wasn't having any of their protests, "It's the 18th day since he came here. You have to give me a timeline to discharge him. 2 days, 4 days, 6 days – what will it be?"

"Look, we cannot guarantee anything including the fact whether he'll ever be okay or not," they tried to pacify her.

However, she was beyond livid now. She decided enough was enough, and said, "Fine. Discharge him, I'll take him home and keep him under my care."

"That isn't a good idea," they tried to warn her, "Taking him home right now isn't going to be easy. You'll have to sign documents and an undertaking as well – that this is completely your decision to take him. And it wasn't under our advisement."

"I'll sign it," she grumbled, having lost her faith and patience in the doctors and the hospital, "Just give me the patient, I'll take him home and make him better again."

She signed the forms and took Karan in a wheelchair. He vaguely remembered that when his mother-in-law, his brother, and his father, had come to get him from the hospital, some of the doctors were looking at him. Other nurses followed them to ensure he was okay. Everyone thought they wouldn't survive. Maata ji took him to her home.

"I'll take care of my son-in-law now. You can go home. Do not worry, he'll be fine again," she told my father and brother, determinedly.

Karan rested. The doctors had prescribed medicine. One of them even shared his personal number – saying if there was an emergency then Maata ji should give him a call. The line was open 24/7. The doctor didn't believe for a second Karan would make it alive once he was out of the hospital premises. But Maata ji had been adamant. There was no arguing with her over trying to keep Karan there for even one more day. Karan, for his own part, was thankful that he could get out of the stifling hospital atmosphere. Once he came back to his mother-in-law's place, he experienced another miracle.

***

He was sleeping in the bed, the same room as the kids, but on his own bed next to them. His father-in-law and mother-in-law were sleeping in another room. It was the month of October and the weather was pleasantly cool. He wanted to feel that cool breeze on himself. Because, for too long, he had been cooped up in the centrally airconditioned hospital!

He told Maata ji, "I have stayed in the air-conditioned hospital for too long. Please open the doors and windows, because I want the outside cool air to come in."

Maata ji didn't argue with him. She happily obliged. To her, Karan asking for anything for himself was a sign of his improving health. He hadn't been able to ask even for a glass of water when he had been in the hospital. There had been too many things sticking to him to even allow him the room to breathe on his own, much less ask for anything. Karan's little requests were giving her some hope that he would eventually pull through a make a full recovery.

Karan too wanted nothing more than to stop feeling this way. Of course, he no longer wanted the end to come the way he'd wished during that fatal night. But even with his request, his discomfort never quite went away. He just wanted to feel okay again. He didn't think that was too much to ask for himself. Maata ji had opened the windows and doors as per his request. But it still didn't feel comfortable enough for him. A familiar sense of hopelessness gripped him.

Once again, he thought this was perhaps the end – but then remembering his kids, he prayed to god again, asking him to do something that would make him well again. This time, he didn't argue or bargain. He just prayed, again not knowing if those prayers would be answered.

Hardly had he finished praying when a gust of cold wind came in from outside. It touched his head, and he felt instantly relieved. He slept off in peace. The next day, he woke up at 9 am. He said, "Maata ji, will you give me a tall glass of water?"

It was the first time in days – the 19th day to be precise – that he drank water. Then he got up and announced he was going to go take a stroll in the garden. While he was strolling a call from the junior doctor came, he wanted to know if Karan was alright. He really didn't believe that Karan would survive the night. He had called, fearing the worst. But what he heard left him in stunned silence.

"Karan is absolutely fine now," Maata ji told the bewildered junior doctor.

"Can I speak to him?" the doctor asked, shocked.

"No, that's not possible right now. He's gone to take a stroll in the park."

The junior doctor was stunned by this revelation and said, "If he's fine, then bring him back in 2 days' time. We'll remove the pipes and the staples."

They did exactly that after calling a taxi. At the hospital, everyone was surprised and overjoyed to see Karan, alive and well, and even hugged him tight. And the nurses were in tears, crying, and saying "Sir, you've been saved! And we kept thinking the worst possible things. Then the doctors told us you're coming to get your stitches cut today." I was touched to see how many of the hospital staff cared about my well-being.

Those 18 days of his life were exceptionally hard. And once he had even given up, and almost committed suicide. He had never experienced such darkness. Grief makes you go into extremely dark places in your mind. His health failed him, so soon after the death of his wife, and almost pushed him to his breaking point. But luckily, he remembered in time that he had more to live for in life. His children needed him. And he couldn't very well abandon them just because he had suddenly been inconvenienced by life.

But he would like to reiterate that suicide isn't a solution - it's just a permanent solution for a temporary problem. And even though Karan survived, he wasn't the same as before - he didn't have as much energy, and his body, his figure - everything was gone. Mentally and physically, he had become a zero at this point in time! His graph at this point in time had come down.

It would be months before he could make a full recovery. But for that moment, looking at the faces of his children, he decided this was a battle worth fighting. He would get back to his original health eventually. Right now, he was just happy he was still here – alive, and able to take care of his family.

***

CHAPTER - SIX

They say that the idle mind is the devil's workshop. After being bedridden for so long and taking longer to recover, Karan began to feel restless about being at home for two months straight! He wanted to get back out there. But he had lost almost twenty kilos! His body was no longer functioning as well as used to before. He realized there was a high chance that he would never be able to go back to the construction industry again. It required a lot of energy, high motivation, and a lot of hard work. A part of him believed that he would perhaps never be able to get back to that level again. But it was also impossible to let go of the industry that had become deeply ingrained in his very being!

Karan knew he had to start earning again – especially because his kids were dependent on him. However, he knew that it would be impossible to get back to his previous roles where he spent most of his time abroad, looking into projects on-site. Right now, he is a single parent. His sense of responsibility prevented him from going after jobs as he had previously.

Back then it had been different. It was a two-parent household. He could easily go to work, while his wife took care of the kids. Now, he would have to be both the winner and the one instilling discipline for the kids. He wondered how he would manage to juggle both roles together. Especially, if he ended up being posted at far-flung places again. His kids had grown used to his presence at home. How were they going to adjust to him being gone again? Would they be fine with not having either parent around? A thousand and one worries plagued Karan's mind. He reminded himself that he was still thinking about going back to work. He didn't know what would happen next. He decided that he would seek the counsel of the one person who would also give him sound advice and not just tell him what he wanted to hear.

"Mata ji," Karan said, one morning, as he sipped his morning chai in the living room of his in-laws' house, "I am thinking of going back to work again."

"Of course," she said, at once, "I think you should definitely get back out there."

"But it has to be an office job," Karan said, more to himself than to her, "I can't leave the kids alone. I'm all they have right now. Plus, I don't think my body can take the strain of doing the rigorous physical activities I was doing previously."

"Well," she said, gently, "They do have us too. I'll look after them. You go look for jobs."

With her blessing, Karan decided to start job hunting. He found a walk-in interview at a company for someone who would be their billing cum planning engineer. While this company catered to my sector, he knew he was way overqualified for this job. Still, reminding himself that beggars could not be choosers, he went to this interview.

***

In the office waiting room, Karan noticed that the other candidates were significantly younger than he was. Determined to not let that bother him, he took my place and waited for his turn. The receptionist there gave everyone there a rather lengthy form to fill out. It was almost 8 to 10 pages long. Having been in the habit of writing fast, Karan ended up breezing through the entire form. He attached his resume to it and handed it back to the receptionist.

But instead of being impressed, the receptionist was downright annoyed with him. He couldn't believe that Karan was just that capable of the task given to him. Sometimes, being young makes you arrogant it seems.

"How did you manage to fill up your form this quickly?" the receptionist asked him, startled, "Are you sure you want to be here?"

"I've always been in the habit of writing really fast," Karan explained, patiently, "You can flip through the pages. I've filled in everything that you've asked me to."

Scowling, the receptionist took the form and flicked through it. He looked a little pleased when he found what he believed was an error. "Aha! See here? In the space of spouse, you wrote not applicable! What do you mean by that? I don't think you're remotely serious about getting a job here. Are you absolutely sure you want to be here?"

"Sir," Karan said, still holding on to his patience, "My wife passed away. I didn't think it was relevant anymore to put her information in for you. What purpose would it solve for you anyway? You cannot really contact her in case of an emergency now, can you?"

"Oh, I am so terribly, terribly sorry," the receptionist said, horrified as what Karan had just said sunk into him. "I really, truly am. Please wait here."

The receptionist's smug look quickly changed into one that was utterly horrified. He apologized profusely for making such an insensitive comment and began flicking through the pages of Karan's form and resume. He disappeared into one of the backrooms for a bit right after. Karan wondered why people just assumed the worst instead of asking things first. He believed the receptionist's bad attitude was due to his lack of experience. So, he just shook his head at the whole exchange. Just a minute of kindness would have prevented this whole ordeal, he thought. He did as he was asked, and Karan waited patiently for his turn for the interview.

***

"Our director and our general manager want to meet you," the receptionist said when he emerged from the backroom a few minutes later. "This way please."

"Oh, but why?" Karan began to ask. Nevertheless, he got up and followed the receptionist to a conference room.

The director and general manager of the company were seated on one side of the long table. Karan took his place opposite them.

"Hello," he said, politely.

"Hello," the direction said, kindly, "Before we start anything – I'm curious to know – why did you apply for such a low position at our firm?"

"Because," Karan explained, for what felt like the hundredth time to him, "I am a single parent to two small kids. I need an office job to cater to their needs. And I need the money to make ends meet."

"We understand that, of course," the general manager said, smiling at him. "We are a very small company and we're thrilled that someone like you – who's worked in companies thrice as big as we are – was still willing to come here and interview with us."

"Yes," the director agreed, "but that being said, I'm sorry, Karan, we cannot give you the position you've applied for. You do realize you're overqualified for it?"

"However," the general manager said, "We are able to offer you a different position. It will require you to travel to South Asian countries though."

"Sir," Karan said, slowly, "I just told you I am a single parent to two small children. I cannot leave them and go anywhere. It's kind of you to consider me, but right now the kids need me more."

"What if you had to go there for only 10 days out of the month, every month?" the director pressed on, "We would like you to go there and just negotiate the deals with our clients on our behalf. That's doable right?"

"Sir, my kids just lost their mother," Karan said, softly, "I hope you understand I don't want to leave them with a feeling that their father is abandoning them too. Even if it's to put food on their plates."

"Then we have nothing more to discuss, Karan," the director said, sighing, "Because we cannot hire you for the position you've applied for. It'll be severely unfair to you and to us."

"But please remember, if you ever change your mind about joining our company, please let us know. Our doors will always be open for you," the general manager added.

Karan thanked them for their time and left. On his way back home, he reflected on the fact that sometimes it was a really bad thing to have as much experience as he did. He had rendered himself unqualified for the jobs he would be able to do at the time. And, he would have to take a huge pay cut. Neither seemed like a good option to him.

He closed his eyes and prayed. Whatever happened would happen for the best. For now, at least he and his kids were together. They might not be happy yet – but they had each other.

He knew the gods had listened to him once and he was confident they would listen to him again. Whatever was best for his family would eventually unfold. There was little he could do worrying about not having the job that he wanted currently.

***

There were advertisements playing on the television all the time after the dot com boom. One in particular was for a job portal. It caught Karan's attention. Thinking nothing much would come from it, he uploaded his resume and filled in his details. Soon, he was getting callbacks for interviews!

But Karan's next job didn't come from the job portal or from newspaper listings. It came from an old acquaintance who was also an engineer. He called Karan to inquire if he was up for taking up a job in a far-flung small town in Maharashtra, called Ahmad Nagar.

"It's a really small town," his friend explained over the phone, "Small construction. It's not a big project at all. In fact, you're going to go there as a consultant and not a project manager."

"Let me think about it," Karan said and decided to take his mother-in-law's counsel before making any major decisions.

***

"I think you should take the job," Mataji told him, firmly, "You're getting restless sitting at home. Let the children stay here with me. I'll look after them while you're gone."

"But I'll still be gone," Karan tried to protest, "The whole reason for looking for an office job was to make sure the kids don't feel alone."

"They aren't alone," Mataji countered, "They have me, they have their Dadaji. They are going to school. They have their friends. You need to get back to work. You'll still be in India. So, here's a start. Right?"

The woman's logic was impeccable. Karan couldn't argue with her. He accepted that this was what he would do for the next few months before he could figure out what his next logical step would be. This time around, Karan didn't enjoy his work or staying in a new city as much. Perhaps he missed his kids, perhaps he knew the price he paid for the life he now had. He couldn't wait for the project to get over so that he could go back to his family again.

***

Nothing makes you more miserable than self-pity. Karan had been feeling bad for himself all the time he had been working in Ahmad Nagar – until, he went to Beed. While he had his fair share of troubles, something he discovered here, shook him to his very core.

During the time he was helping with the water treatment plant, the place was going through a horrible drought. It was a bad time for everyone in the villages as well. Everyone there was working in

83

the sugar cane field and got paid daily wages. This invariably meant that the minute someone didn't show up for work, their fees for that day would get deducted.

For women, it meant living through hell, because their menstrual cycles would keep them from working at least 3 to 5 days in the month! It was then that Karan discovered a lot of these women were choosing to remove their uterus. He was horrified by their choices.

"But it's literally between being at home, not earning money, and suffering," the women reasoned, "And not having to deal with our menstrual cycle and going to work every day of the month!"

Karan closed his eyes and prayed to his god. "Thank you for showing me that while I have been through a horrible time – there are people who are forced with two equally horrible choices. You have taught me a really valuable lesson. And for that, I am grateful."

He promised that wouldn't feel miserable and sad about life, but try to make the most of it. Some part of it still couldn't believe that in the day and age they were in, women had to give up such a huge part of themselves just to survive the world. He shook his head and prayed – hopefully, there will be a better tomorrow.

***

During this time, when Karan was away from his family—his mother-in-law, his children, and, of course, his wife—he began to reflect on his past.

Memories that he had long tucked away resurfaced in the quiet loneliness of the nights. His mind drifted back to his college days, to the laughter, the camaraderie, and the fleeting moments that shaped him. Among those memories, one stood out: Maya.

Maya was a striking woman, a fellow engineering student, though she was in a different department. Karan, a Civil Engineering student, admired her from a distance. In those days, it was uncommon to see women in engineering, and Maya was not just any woman—she was beautiful, and intelligent, and radiated a warmth that drew people to her. The men in their batch considered themselves fortunate to share classes with her. Yet, Karan knew his place. He admired her quietly, never daring to express his feelings. The barriers of faith and tradition were too high to cross. Maya was from a Sikh family, while Karan belonged to a Hindu household. Interfaith relationships were frowned upon, and Karan was too practical to dream of a life with her.

He eventually moved on, met his wife, and lived a happy life, or so he thought. But now, with his wife gone and his children living their own lives, Karan found himself questioning the choices he had made. As he lay awake at night, the thought of Maya crept into his mind. "What if I had told her?" he wondered. "Would things have been different?"

He knew it was pointless to dwell on such thoughts, yet he couldn't help but let his mind wander. He imagined what life might have been like if he and Maya had defied the odds if they had braved societal constraints and built a life together. Would their families have accepted them? Would Maya have been a good wife, a loving mother, and a dutiful daughter-in-law? And more importantly, would she have been there with him now, easing the loneliness that engulfed him?

The questions swirled in his mind, but deep down, he knew the answers didn't matter. The past was the past, and the life he had lived was the one he was meant to live. Yet, as he lay in the dark, he allowed himself to indulge in the fantasy, picturing a domestic life filled with warmth and love—a life where he wasn't so alone. Perhaps it was the solitude that made these thoughts surface, the ache of missing someone who could never return.

Karan sighed heavily. He had never once regretted his decision to marry his wife, and never felt the need to revisit his feelings for Maya. His marriage had given him years of joy and two wonderful children. But in these quiet moments, when the world around him was silent, he couldn't help but wonder about the road not taken.

"Some stories are like that," Karan mused to himself as sleep finally began to calm him. "They don't begin, they don't end—they just linger in the corners of our minds."

He wondered, fleetingly, if Maya ever thought of him, if she remembered him at all. It was a foolish notion, he knew. But as he hummed an old tune to himself, he let the thought drift away. When morning came, he would return to his work, his thoughts of Maya lost once more to the demands of the day. For now, he would sleep, and let the memories rest where they belonged—in the past.

CHAPTER - SEVEN

The project that Karan was a part of in Bheed in Maharashtra was a small one. While the incidents he faced there were quite traumatizing, as time passed, he noticed things began to improve. The good news was that his health was slowly getting better as well. The thought that at least he was still in India, and could go back to his family at the drop of a hat, helped Karan get through this particular project. He still hadn't given up on his initial determination to make sure he found a job that would help him not only provide – but also give his children a happy and comfortable life.

So, when he wasn't on-site working, he would browse jobs online. Karan's profile on the job portal continued to attract the attention of several companies. He began to get offers from a lot of really good companies. He was happy that life was finally beginning to look up again. Especially from abroad. But due to his original plan of staying near to his family, at least initially, Karan had to skip most of these inquiries.

But when Fate has a plan for you, there's little to nothing you can do about it. One such job that stood out for him came from East Africa. It was planning for a town that needed a sewerage and water network system. They offered Karan quite a good position with good pay. To him, it felt like a no-brainer to accept the offer. So, he accepted the offer, of course. But he knew he needed to consult his family – his children, and Maata ji before he actually left for another country halfway around the world. He asked the company to give him a month before he needed to join them. He immediately quit the job that he had in Maharashtra and came back home.

When he came home, the kids were delighted to see him. Maata ji was happy that he was back home. But Karan knew he needed to have a difficult conversation with them.

"I have been offered a position abroad," Karan told his children, "And since it's a really good opportunity, I have decided to take it on."

"Alright," his children chimed up.

They were used to their father going on long work trips. They had always looked forward to his return. While they missed their mother, they had grown used to living with their grandparents. For their grandparents, it was a way to stop missing their daughter so much. They would have missed the kids and have nothing left to live for, had Karan decided to move out on his own, and take the kids with him.

"Yes," Maata ji said, "You know the kids are fine here. They have settled down well into these lives of theirs. New school, new friends – and no one is looking at them with pity as they were in the other place. They got their fresh start. You deserve one too."

"Thank you, Maata ji," Karan said, gratefully.

He was looking forward to going back to a job he really loved and was qualified for. He had tried his hand at other work – but they didn't give him the happiness or the satisfaction that he had before. Plus, the monetary aspect too didn't help at all. He knew all too well he had been overqualified for half the jobs that were available closer to home. It was time to face the music and do what was best for himself – because that was what would be the best thing for his family.

He focused on the next thing: which was his project. He knew if he did a good job, this would open up opportunities for him in other places as well. This was just a stepping stone back into the world where he truly belonged. A way for him to ensure that his kids got everything that they wanted from this life.

He packed his bags, bid his family farewell, and boarded the plane that took him to his next adventure. His stomach was in knots. Because while he was thrilled at the chance to get back to his work again, he was a little apprehensive about going so far away this time around. The memories from the last time he had been too far away from his family were fresh in his mind. He never wanted to be in a position where when tragedy struck his family, it would take him three whole days to get back! Especially when the circumstances were absolutely beyond his control.

Karan settled into his airplane seat and leaned back. So far, Hanuman ji has ensured that he was leading a good, healthy, and stable life. During his life-or-death moment, he had chosen to trust god more than himself. So said a quick prayer and once again put his fate in the hands of god. He would trust that no matter what life decided to throw at him now, he would come out of it absolutely fine.

The air hostess had started their routine of letting everyone know about flight safety. They insisted, "Please put your own oxygen masks on before assisting your children with theirs." He had never thought about this before. But right now, it made perfect sense to him. How could he even dream of being there for his kids if he didn't know how to be there for himself? He breathed deeply. He knew instantly then that this was the right decision. Whatever decisions he had made so far, he had kept his kids' wellbeing in mind first. He settled down into his seat and closed his eyes. It's like they said in the movies – everything would be fine in the end. If it wasn't, it just wasn't the end.

***

Karan's next adventure saw him in Tanzania. The project was under the World Bank. This world was completely different from the world he had lived and experienced before. The crime rate was high, there was extreme poverty, and they didn't have access to the most basic things – like healthcare, food nutrition, etc. People there couldn't even afford their meals three times a day.

To Karan's horror, he found that here people were dying of both HIV and Malaria! There were too many people who were HIV+. While he did have a lot of people in the labour force, he had no idea of their medical histories – and how many of the currently working folks might be HIV+! But he was told by his superiors to keep certain precautions. Such as not sharing the same blade for shaving etc. The World Health Organization and other NGOs were quite active there too – especially to teach how to prevent HIV, and how to ensure you live safely, and not spread it, in case the disease got its hands on you.

Karan could still accept HIV being the reason for so many people's deaths. It was, after all, a deadly disease. He couldn't understand why people out there were dying from malaria! That's when he realized that even the most basic medication wasn't available to the people there in Tanzania. But despite these challenging circumstances, the local African people who were labourers, engineers, and supervisors – had really good knowledge when it came to their work. They were good technicians and well-qualified engineers. Naturally, Karan believed at least the education system was strong. It had done its best to churn out students who knew what they were going to do.

Most of them held BTech and MTech degrees. They were well-versed in their work. And Karan was thoroughly impressed by how knowledgeable they all were. After witnessing the circumstances in which they grew up firsthand, it was doubly impressive what these wonderful young men were able to make of themselves.

Karan received special training in how to handle workers who might be HIV+. He also noticed that there was no discrimination between the workers on the basis of their medical history. Neither did anyone out another person, claiming someone might be HIV+. Their brotherhood really did not know any bounds.

One of the most shocking things that Karan witnessed during his project in Tanzania was that outside of the washrooms (both the ones for males and females), there were condom dispensers! In fact, it was mandatory to keep them. This meant no one had to purchase condoms, but they were distributed free of cost, provided by the World Health Organization and other NGOs. In case anyone needed it, they could just go to the washroom, press the button on the dispenser, and get it. There was no shame associated with this. No one would hesitate to get the condoms for the dispensers either.

To Karan, this was a culture shock. Because he remembered that back in India, adults – that too married adults, when they go to the pharmacy to buy condoms, used to feel jittery. They would feel hesitant even if there was a need to feel that way. To him, it was a learning. Condoms are the best way to prevent HIV and other sexually transmitted diseases. It is always a good idea to use them. While Tanzania was behind in many aspects, when it came to making good choices for their sexual well-being – they were lightyears ahead.

The good choices weren't just extended to the public restrooms. Before he joined his site, Karan had been put up in a hotel. He noticed that in the washroom of his hotel room – with the usual supply of toiletries, and soaps and shampoos, there were also condoms. It was clear that they genuinely believed that it was better to be safe than sorry.

It was then that Karan realized that the guests checking in good easily call the front desk, and say, "Hello! Could you send me a toothbrush, a toothpaste – and oh, some condoms too." And the receptionist would reply, "Yes, right away, Sir!" or, "Sure. Right away, Ma'am." He was impressed with the way they had all united to take as many necessary measures as possible to prevent the spread of this deadly disease.

Another thing that stands out about Tanzania – especially during the time Karan had been posted there – was the wild animals who were roaming free. He had noticed them during his trips to the site. They were roaming around, on the sides of roads, without a care in the world. It used to make his heart pound wildly – wondering if they got too close to these creatures and if that day would become his last. He would see zebras, giraffes, and tigers, just minding their own business.

Of course, Karan had grown up going to the zoo and reading about these animals in books. But to see them every day outside of his place of residence without a care in the world, made him feel as though he was actually living out in the pages of *The Jungle Book*. His work had literally taken him around the world and gifted him with utterly surreal experiences. Sometimes, Karan wondered if he had been dreaming the whole time.

He also wondered how a conversation about the wild animals roaming around in front of his house would go with his kids back home.

"How was work today, papa?" his daughter would have asked.

"Oh, I got a little late," he imagined himself saying, "there was an elephant right outside of my door, who refused to move."

He wondered if someone who didn't witness these situations firsthand would actually believe that this was what he had to encounter on a daily basis! Seeing wild animals for a distance was one thing, especially when you were taking part in a safari. But to actually see them every day – and coexist with them was another thing altogether.

Years later, it seems like an amazing adventure. But in that moment, it had felt like anything but. The workers had been scared for their lives. Karan too had to wonder constantly if he would make it out from there alive. He had feared for his life once before when he had been stationed in Afghanistan. Now, while this was a completely different circumstance, he was wondering how truly safe he was in the house that he lived in.

After a while, he was asked to find accommodation closer to the job site. He took a house on rent nearer to the site, and he also hired a driver called Ali. The first night, he woke up and saw that there were elephants and giraffes roaming outside his house. He also noticed two men standing outside, talking to each other. Not feeling easy about what he was seeing, he made the decision to call headquarters the first thing the next day.

"I think I've taken a house too deep inside," Karan told them urgently, "I am waking up to wild animals roaming around. And suspicious characters standing outside my window."

"Alright," they replied, "We will take care of it immediately."

That turned out to be giving him a security guard – or, a gunman. Karan lived inside the house, and on the outside, his driver and his security guard lived. Some days, he would wake up to find another wild animal roaming outside. He would have to wait until they decided to move before he could take the car out and leave for work. On days when it got too late, his security guard with fire in the air, and noise would send the animals running helter-skelter.

Karan didn't like disrupting the wild animals' natural outings. But given the fact he had to report to a job on time, he didn't have much of a choice. He comforted himself by telling himself that this was all temporary anyway. He would be moving on from there, once the work here was done. The animals would be able to reclaim their land. And hopefully, he would pick up a job at a place where he didn't have to wake up to strange men outside of his doorway, and animals roaming free in his front yard!

He needed to leave his house by 8.30 am, in order to not miss call time. On one such day, as they drove to the site, he noticed children walking barefoot, with schoolbags on their backs. They seemed to be absolutely unbothered by their condition. They were laughing and shouting, talking over one another. Curiosity got the better of Karan. He asked Ali about these children.

"Ali, where are these kids off to?"

"Oh, them," Ali said, "they're walking to school."

"Where's the school?" Karan asked, curiously.

"You know your work site?" Ali said.

"Yes."

"3 km ahead of that."

"And where do these kids live?"

"Further down from where you stay, sir. In the village."

Karan immediately felt horrible for giving God such a hard time about his life. Yes, his life hadn't turned out as he had planned. But he had a beautiful wife until she was called away by God. And he had two amazing children. All his hardships came to him after he had at least reached his adulthood. He had lived a good life – before things began going downhill for him.

Whereas these kids... They hadn't even hit puberty, and they were already facing such a tough life. They had to walk barefoot to school, and again back. He realized they were doing it for their education. Immediately, he wanted to do whatever he could in his power to help out. He had always believed that one should help whenever they can. The help they give out into the universe comes back to you tenfold, all the time.

"Find out where these kids live, Ali."

"Sir? Are you sure about that?"

"Please do as I say."

"Alright, Sir."

Ali did his due diligence and found out where the kids lived. He reported they were all from the village, he lived nearby to. Karan went there and offered to take the kids to school. He made it clear to them that he could only drop them to school.

"Our times for coming back home don't match," he said, kindly, "But I hope we are able to help you just by dropping you off at school every morning."

He changed his car from a Sedan to a Toyota Hilux – which had a loading dock at the back. It would have enough space for ten to twelve children to sit there comfortably. It became a ritual for him. To get up early, get breakfast, get dressed, and pick up the kids, and drop them to school, before coming back to the site to work. Some days, when he wanted to indulge them, he would treat them to cold drinks and on other days sweets. He could tell they were really grateful for him. Karan felt elated being able to do something that was making these kids so very happy.

It was a small act of kindness. But Karan had lived long enough to know about the ripple effect. Even if one person remembered his kindness and paid it forward, it would ensure that things changed for the greater good in the end.

Years later, he still thinks of them and misses them. He got in touch with Ali over the years and asked, "How are the kids doing now?"

"They're all good, Sir. They keep remembering you and missing you." Ali said, happily, "You really did make a difference in their lives."

Karan found out later that even the village head remembered him and had nothing but kind words to say about him.

"There was an Indian boss who had come to our village," the head of the village said, "he saw our children walking barefoot to school, and decided to do something about it. He took care of our children and made sure they knew kindness. Especially, because life can sometimes be very unkind and rather unfair."

The villagers agreed. For the kids, it had been a relief to be driven to school every morning. They could focus on learning and getting better grades. Coming back home walking was fun. They were eager to run back and begin the lessons. Not having to wake up earlier than necessary just to make it in time for school, had been a huge blessing for all of them. These were well-rested kids now going to have a good shot at education. Not kids who were already exhausted by the time they received their first lesson.

Karan lay back in his armchair, as he remembered the kids, in the present day, and smiled to himself. "They must be grown-ups by now," he thought, thinking of the littlest one in the party, "By now, they must have become whoever they wanted to be when they were younger. They must be in their first or second jobs by now."

He missed the kids all the time. He was happy to learn that they missed him all the time too, and kept thinking about him from time to time. Tanzania had a lot of things to offer Karan. But the best ones were the memories – of both living with wild animals in the middle of nowhere and getting to be exactly the person the kids needed when he was there and getting his chance to make a world of difference in someone else's life.

***

CHAPTER - EIGHT

Karan's hard work in Tanzania paid off. Soon, his boss called him to tell him that he was going to be sent to Kenya on another project. He was also a little secretive about his real intentions behind sending Karan to Kenya. This created a sense of intrigue for Karan. He had never been a part of sting operations before. It was new territory for him, but he was feeling excited and exhilarated about it. The director went on to explain what had been going on at the site.

"We'll be sending you there as a site engineer," his boss said.

Immediately, Karan's heart began to hammer. It was not a big post. In fact, it was a much smaller role than what Karan had been playing in Tanzania! Plus, the pay wouldn't be as good. He wanted to protest. How was he getting offered a lower position if he had already proved himself worthy of the company? Then before he could spiral, his boss explained the situation to him.

"We're sending you there on the pretext of being a site engineer. We've received information that the General Manager there has been indulging in all of the activities that are against company policy. We want you to investigate it and report it back to us. You're actually going there to replace him. But if we announce that right now, it'll tip him off and we'll never find out the truth."

Karan readily agreed to this operation. He had never understood why people would be willing to take bribes. He remembered the man from years ago who had tried to steal money from the company, and ended up getting blown up by the land mine! The one who had tried to frame him. Karma was real and it was going to come for everyone in the end. Still, he knew he owed to the people for whom they were building the projects the access to better sewerage systems and water systems. It was horrible to cheat them off things that were rightfully theirs.

"But this is a secret mission, Karan," his boss reminded him again, "So whatever you do, don't blow your cover before you've gathered the evidence."

Even on his way to Kenya, Karan thought about the actions of the General Manager. How was he stealing from things that weren't his? How could he take bribes? And compromising on the qualities of the goods being used for the project? No self-respecting engineering would even think about tarnishing their reputation in such a way!

He kept thinking about the incident from early on in his career in Afghanistan when everyone accused him of stealing from the company. In the end, it turned out the supervisor was the one who had been stealing from the company. He lost his life and got caught in the process. It was a terrible way for the truth to come out. But Karan knew that dishonesty never wins. And the truth finds ways to always come out. Sometimes in the ugliest ways possible!

In order to ensure no one realized Karan's real purpose of being in Kenya, the company told everyone that they were sending Mr. Karan from Tanzania to join them as a site engineer. Karan's moral values and integrity already ensured that he would get to the bottom of this mystery. Determined, he went to the project in Kenya. The General Manager there didn't think for a minute that he had been found out yet. He was more than happy to add another labourer to his force.

***

Karan reached Kenya along with fifty other labourers. They were collected from the airport by the representative there. It was only here that he realized the length of his undercover work. He was about to experience firsthand how the lowly site engineers were treated vis-à-vis the managers and general managers. He had been at the top of the food chain for so long, that he had completely forgotten the way the ones at the bottom were treated.

"Get on the bus, all of you," the representative barked at them, after scanning their documents and making sure everything was in order.

Karan looked at the tiny bus expected to fit all fifty of them and approached him. "I'm an engineer. Isn't there a car available for me?"

"Everyone up till the engineers and senior engineers have to take the bus," the representative said, rudely, "You're just a site engineer. You can either take the bus. Or, if you want to use your brains so much – I can give you the address and you can book a cab to the place by yourself."

Furious at being spoken to in such an ill manner, Karan angrily opened his mouth to tell the representative off. Then he remembered his conversation with the director. He was supposed to pretend to be a site engineer and investigate the matter, before replacing the current General Manager. He couldn't very well blow his cover by telling the man in front of him off, and warning him to be careful – because eventually he'd become his boss. The man would find that out in due time and live to regret not showing basic human decency.

They stopped for lunch on the way. It was a horrible place. Karan was in shock thinking this was where the labourers were expected to have their lunch! He went to the HR representative and said, "Are you serious? Why are you making us eat out here? It's super unhygienic. Take us some other place."

"Can you stop being so over-smart?" the other man, named Rakesh, spat, "You don't get it do you? The company isn't going to spend more money on the labourers such as yourself! This is what's there in the budget. You can either eat here, or the next meal you'll get is in the office."

Irritated, Karan pushed down his meal. He knew he had to go through this ordeal in order to come out of the other side triumphantly. He took a deep breath, and waited for the time to come when he could put this rude HR in his place!

After his meal, he went to meet the General Manager. This man's name was Mahesh. Mahesh had come there from Gujrat. He had no idea that the company had caught wind of what he'd been secretly doing over the last few months. He seemed absolutely sure that he had gotten away with his deception.

"Hello," Karan said, pleasantly, standing in front of him, "I'm Karan. I was recently transferred here from Tanzania. I'll be joining your team as a site engineer."

"Hmm," Mahesh said, without getting up from his seat, or offering Karan a seat, "It's good to have you here."

He went into describing the job to Karan, and what would be expected of him. But Karan was already suspicious of the man in front of him. He genuinely didn't believe the labourers deserved to be treated equally, and it showed in his behaviour. Karan had no problem believing that this man was capable of being dreadfully evil! He had been alive long enough to know that it was the little things that gave away a man's true nature. If they had known who he really was, they would been bending over backwards trying to accommodate him – making sure he was taken care of well. But since they had dismissed Karan as just a mere labourer – he couldn't expect better treatment than the one that he was being currently given.

Karan thought about the proverb, money talks but wealth whispers, and realized what an apt saying it was. Mahesh and Rakesh had no problem throwing around their weight because the positions in their company had already made it easy for them. They were stealing money from the company and thought that this was their get-rich-quick scheme – and no one had to be wiser about it. Karan wondered why they thought they were going to get away with it.

"Come to the site from tomorrow," Mahesh said, "Looking forward to seeing all the good work you do for us."

It annoyed Karan. The way this man spoke to him, the way the HR representative kept dismissing him because of the position he held in the company. He had to start building his case – and fast. So, the next day when he went to the site, he didn't waste any time befriending the other labourers in the field. And while there was a huge age difference between them, it didn't stop them from being candid with him.

"I've heard rumours that General Manager has been doing certain things that he shouldn't be doing," Karan asked, curiously to one of his co-workers, "Is there any truth to this?"

"Yes," one of them said, "He's ordered materials that aren't as good as the quality as they should be. It's horrible. We know it's wrong and we can't do much about it."

"He's the boss after all," another one chimed up, "And you know how that goes. We'll lose our jobs if we dare try to contradict him!"

Karan let out a deep breath. He especially hated people who took advantage of the weak because of the positions of power they were in. He visited the local police station too, hoping it would shed some light on the ongoings in the Kenya project. He realized that Mahesh had managed to siphon off millions of dollars without any trace!

Armed with the proof the director had been looking for, Karan gave him a call, and said, "Your suspicions are correct. Mahesh has been manhandling everything here. And I have the proof to back up your beliefs and my claims."

"That's really good work, Karan," the director said, "Now, I want you to take over his place. You do what is necessary to replace him on the spot there as the General Manager of the Kenya project. You have our go-ahead. And we'll start the announcement here from our end too."

"Sounds good, boss," Karan said and hung up.

He smiled. He had wondered before how Mahesh had thought no one knew what he was up to. Karan wondered who the original whistleblower had been and if they had been justly rewarded for their hard work. But he knew one thing - Karma really did come for everyone, in the end, he realized.

***

Armed with a daring plan, Karan waited for the next day to come. When he went to work, he was on the lookout for the chance to put his plan into action. Once the General Manager had gone into the site for his inspection, he quietly sat down at the General Manager's chair in the office. This started a flurry of events. It made everyone from the peon to the HR manager, to the other co-workers, stare at him as though he had lost his mind!

"How dare you sit at the General Manager's desk?" the HR yelled at him.

"Sir, you cannot be sitting here. It's not your place," the peon too said, scared about what would happen next.

Calmly Karan told them, "You might have received an email already – or will receive one in the next ten minutes – which will explain to you why I'm sitting at this desk. I'm the new General Manager. Mr. Mahesh's replacement. I am not the site engineer that you have been thinking I was."

While he said this the mail arrived in everyone's inboxes. It also told them that Mr. Mahesh was being terminated from his position effective immediately. Mr. Karan was the new boss, and everyone had to report to him. It made the HR Representative, Rakesh, go red in the face. He realized the blunder that he had made! But there was no going back. Everyone started whispering about Mr. Mahesh's termination – and how all the rumours they had heard were true.

A weird-looking local guy appeared at the office and said, "I'm looking for Mr. Mahesh. I've been given strict instructions to take him to the airport and ensure he's deported. His termination is effective immediately, after all. He cannot be here at all. His ticket is ready too. Where is he?"

Mr. Mahesh was escorted off the site, under the watchful eyes of Karan. He then turned to Rakesh, who was standing in his office, and told him coldly, "You're supposed to be the HR. You have the power to make a difference. And yet, since I've got here – I've only seen you make very poor choices. You're supposed to help people who are here – away from their families and loved ones. But you leave no chance to belittle them and make them feel bad about themselves. You have been treating the people as third-class citizens!"

"Sir, please," he pleaded, "I didn't have any idea who you were."

"That's not the point. You shouldn't treat me badly, just because you think I hold a lower position in the company," Karan said, firmly, "Besides – I have experienced firsthand what you have done. I've seen the cost of the meals we were served after taking the bus. While I understand the bus, I don't understand why you would make everyone eat at such a low-cost, horrible place. Or rather, I didn't understand it until I saw the invoices you had raised for the same expense."

Rakesh looked like a deer caught in the headlights. He had committed a crime and now there was no escaping it. And worst of all, the new General Manager had a firsthand account of his horrible crime.

"The invoice is three times higher than what you spend, Mr. Rakesh," Karan said, coldly, "I will be well within my right to fire you on the spot. Especially as the General Manager and your boss."

Immediately Rakesh fell to his knees, and grabbing Karan's feet, pleaded, "Please, Sir. I've made a mistake. It won't happen again. I'm really sorry."

"Sorry, you got caught, or sorry you treated the labourers like third-class citizens? You do realise that you have essentially stolen from the labourers? They are entitled to good quality meals. On paper, you are showing you've provided that for them. But we both know you've not done that in real life, and pocketed the difference." Karan asked him.

"Sir, please," Rakesh continued, pleading, "I didn't know better. It won't happen again."

"Hmm," Karan said, analysing the situation, "I won't terminate your contract yet. You are far away from your family too. And you have a job to do. You better do it well, and let that be the last mistake you ever make. Because if I ever catch you doing anything as bad as this one – that'll be your last day with us. You're the HR – you're supposed to ensure the employees receive fair treatment. You've just abused your power. I want you to think about what you've done and understand that there can be severe consequences for your actions going forward."

Karan let off Rakesh with a warning because he realized Rakesh was young and naïve. He was barely twenty-seven or twenty-eight years old. He still had a lot to learn about the world. He had already learned his first lesson – never assume everything that you see is real. He had dismissed Karan thinking he was a lowly site engineer and soon found out that he was the new boss! Never again was he going to assume things. And he wasn't going to cheat the poor labourers out of good meals either. Happy with how the day turned out, Karan turned his attention towards the project in Kenya. He knew he would have to undo a lot of damage that his predecessor had made.

For one thing, he knew he had to replace the cheap quality materials. He couldn't have the workers make constructions out of the horrible material that had been ordered. It would take him some time, but he knew he would be able to pull it off. The first priority he had was to ensure that everyone was safe – even after their work was complete. He didn't want to read about collapses years later after their work had been finished.

***

CHAPTER - NINE

While Karan's work life was thriving, his home life suddenly took another turn. His kids were growing up. They had begun to understand that their mother was gone, but they realized that their father had also gone to a foreign land for his job. Their attachment to their father began to grow stronger. Even Karan began to miss his children a lot.

"I am in a good position in life finally. My health has improved too," Karan thought to himself, "I can indulge my children finally and ensure our bonds remain unbroken."

Since he knew he had reached a certain position in work and life, he was able to take vacations after two to three months and visit his children for a week or so. Whenever he would be posted in safer countries – he would ask his children to come down and visit him too. They would be accompanied by their maternal grandmother i.e. Maata ji. Because for Karan it was important but to keep the bonds between them intact. He needed to nourish and nurture the bond between himself and his son, and himself and his daughter. He didn't want them to become strangers who were just connected to each other by blood. Because familial bonds were what was the most important thing in the world.

He didn't even know where the time flew by during those years. Karan's job took him to more places around the world – such as Mozambique, Uganda, and Zimbabwe.

***

In Zimbabwe, Karan had a huge staff consisting of both technical and non-technical personnel. Among all of his men, he noticed one particular senior engineer, Mr. Kailash. Karan had a hunch that this man wasn't very happy about something. He was sure that he had some problem that was bothering him.

"Mr. Kailash, are you alright?" Karan asked him when he had a chance to have a one-on-one with him.

"Yes, Sir, of course," Kailash replied, without missing a beat.

"Really? Because your face tells me a different story." Karan pressed on.

"No, Sir. You must be mistaken when you see my face." He said and excused himself.

Karan wasn't convinced. He inquired from the others about Kailash. One of the staff members who had been there for some time said, "Oh, he's married but doesn't have any kids. And he hasn't gone home to India in five years."

"Five years?" Karan shrieked. It had killed him when they hadn't let him go home to see his wife for almost two weeks, he remembered weakly. He wondered if the previous manager had been as cruel enough not to allow leaves. "Didn't the previous manager allow leaves?"

"No, Sir," the staff member said, "the mid-level guys are allowed time off. Kailash doesn't want to go home by his choice. None of us really know why."

Finally, Karan decided to corner Kailash during one of his breaks and asked him, "If you want to go home for a bit, I'll sanction your leave."

"No, Sir," Kailash said, firmly, "Thank you, but I don't want any leaves."

"Okay, then I'll make an offer for you. And if you refuse that is your right." Karan said. Having had his share of bad bosses, he was determined to be a better boss and ensure he was making a difference in the lives of the people he was encountering.

"Yes, Sir?" Kailash asked, apprehensive of the offer.

"I'll arrange for your family to come down here and be with you for some time. It cannot be easy to go five years without seeing them. Isn't it?" Karan asked, kindly.

"Sir, no," Kailash said, firmly, "Thank you for being so kind. But I don't want them to come down here at all."

"Okay, now you've lost me," Karan said, exasperatedly, "You don't want to go home. You don't want to see your wife or your family. I don't understand you at all."

"Sir," Kailash said, softly, "I'd gone home for a week, five years ago. After I got back, I came to know that my wife had an extramarital affair. And add insult to injury, it was with a family member."

Whatever Karan had been expecting Kailash to see, it wasn't this. He wondered how many other people were suffering due to unfaithful and negligent spouses similar to that of Kailash.

"If go to my village, how do I show my face there? Everyone knows about the affair. And how do I greet my wife here – as if nothing has happened?" he said, almost in tears. "It's heartbreaking to think she would do something like this. I haven't been able to forgive her. I feel if we see each other – I'll either end up killing her or I'll kill myself. Neither of these are good options."

Karan stayed silent. He knew no words could comfort Kailash. This was his cross to bear, and he was allowed to deal with it as he saw fit. To Karan, he couldn't imagine someone being unfaithful. Especially when the other person was moving heaven and earth, trying to provide a good quality of life for them.

"Sir, it's a good thing I have a job so far away from home," Kailash said, bitterly, "it gives me the perfect excuse to not go home and avoid unnecessary drama."

The Power of Perseverance

Karan and Kailash sat by the tranquil riverside, their conversation taking on a deeper, more reflective tone. Karan looked at Kailash, sensing the turmoil within his friend. He knew this was a moment where words could offer more than just comfort—they could inspire.

"Kailash," Karan began, "sometimes circumstances in life are opposite and adverse to our desires. We must fight for what we believe in, never give up, and never lose hope. Trust in the almighty God. Let me tell you a story I once heard from a wise man."

Kailash listened intently as Karan began his tale.

Once, in a small village, there lived an old and poor man who struggled with a painful and untreatable wound on his cheek. The wound was a deep, festering hole, oozing pus and blood. Doctors had given up, declaring it incurable. Whenever the old man tried to eat, the food would come out through the hole, causing him immense pain and embarrassment.

His family, relatives, siblings, and all the villagers were heartbroken by his suffering. They pleaded with God, asking for an end to his life to relieve him from his pain. But the old man held on, hoping for a miracle.

One morning, as the old man sat outside his house, he watched two bulls fighting. The bulls were muscular, with large, intimidating horns, locked in combat for over an hour. The villagers watched from a distance, knowing that interfering in such a fight could be fatal.

Suddenly, in the midst of their battle, the bulls moved closer to the old man. In a dramatic turn of events, one of the bulls struck the old man's cheek with its horn. The force of the blow tore a piece of flesh from the wound, causing severe bleeding. The villagers rushed the old man to the hospital, fearing the worst.

To everyone's astonishment, a few days later, the wound began to heal. The doctors conducted tests and discovered that the blow from the bull had removed the cancerous tissue. The old man, once resigned to a life of pain, was now completely healed. He was declared fit and fine by the medical team.

Karan paused, letting the story sink in. Kailash was visibly moved, tears welling up in his eyes.

"It is easy to run into a problem," Karan said softly, "but it is hard to keep running away from it. What is happiness? When we accept a situation, that is happiness. When we are unable to accept a situation, that is sadness. It is up to us to choose acceptance and happiness over rejection and sadness."

Kailash broke down, tears streaming down his face. He hugged Karan tightly, crying for a long time. "Thank you, Sir," Kailash whispered, his voice choked with emotion. "You have motivated me more than I can express. I will go back home, meet my child, and return to my birthplace. I will face my problems and resolve them."

Karan smiled, knowing that his words had reached Kailash's heart. Sometimes, all it takes is a story and a few wise words to reignite the flame of hope and perseverance in someone's life.

He walked away, leaving Karan feeling horrible. He knew why Kailash looked troubled all the time, but he couldn't do anything to make things better. He let out a deep sigh. On the surface, people could say they were fine and things were great. But it was only after spending some quality time with each other, that one could understand what was really going on. And sometimes, getting to the bottom of a mystery didn't solve the hurt. It just made it hurt worse.

***

CHAPTER - TEN

After his work in Zimbabwe, Karan got the opportunity to work in several other countries across the world, on many different projects thanks to his experience and expertise. He was reaping the benefits of being in a top position for sure. To name a few he managed projects in Africa, Kenya, Mozambique, Uganda, Southern Africa, Ukraine, Jordan, Egypt, Georgia, Belarus, and the list never stopped.

He happily traveled around the world. He got to be a part of a lot of changes that were made in this world. He felt happy knowing that he had put his engineering degree to good use. Once, he had no idea what he was going to do after his graduation was over. Now, here he was – working globally and making a difference. It made him deeply satisfied with all the decisions he had made in his youth that had landed him in this position.

His kids were also growing up. He continued his tradition of seeing his family once every four months. He would go back home for a week, spend as much time with them as he could, and go back to his projects. Time was flying by for Karan. He had settled into his new role as a single, working dad. And because time is the best healer – the pain and the hurt from the past started to ease up. Of course, he never forgot about it…but the wounds began to heal. He knew the scars would remain forever, as reminders of not what had happened but how he had eventually triumphed over!

He began to slowly entertain the idea that perhaps it would be bad to have someone in his life as well. He thought that eventually his kids would grow up and move into lives of their own. They wouldn't need him quite as much as they needed him right now. What was he going to do when the last of his birds flew out of the nest? Throw himself into more work? Come home to an empty and cold house? He shuddered to think what would happen well into the future. It didn't seem like the worst idea in the world to have someone with him at this point in time.

It was around this time that Karan thought of remarriage. It had been years since his wife had passed away. He knew both he and his kids had moved on. It seemed like the perfect time for him to find a partner and enjoy the rest of his life. While Karan's days were filled with work, it was the nights that were the hardest. A life partner, he knew, was someone he could share all his thoughts and feelings with – without the fear of judgement. He was beginning to feel a little isolated. Because while he had his kids and of course, Maata ji, there were things he knew he would be able to share only with a partner. The kids were too young. And Maata ji had already done more than her share in helping him out. He didn't want to burden her with the position of a confidante as well. Finding someone to share his life with seemed to him to be the next logical step.

"It's time then," Karan told himself, as he reflected on how he wanted to spend the rest of his life, "There should be someone for sure – to share this life with. Or else, the loneliness will kill me."

He knew he would have to take action if he wanted to go through with his remarriage. He opened a profile on one of the online portals for remarriage in India. To make his chances better, he opted for a paid membership for the same. He started looking for his life partner online. But he didn't get many responses. Or rather, he didn't get responses that spoke to him. The ones who did reach out didn't seem genuine to him at all. Nevertheless, he didn't give up and hoped someday he'd find the one he was looking for.

Rumi had once said that what you seek is seeking you. Soon, Karan would have enough evidence to see for himself that what he had been seeking – was indeed seeking him out too!

***

During this time, Karan was posted in South Africa. He was engrossed in a survey that would help him with a bridge that he was constructing. Native to South Africa was a snake that was highly dangerous – the Black Mamba.

When they had to survey the jungle, it was always the Civil Engineers and the team, who would go to the ground first for any other developmental work to come through. They would be exposed to the risks – which meant, they had taken extra precautions for themselves. Since they were going to be dealing in the wild it was obvious they would at some point encounter snakes etc.

Before the work had officially begun, they had been given an induction. They had been warned about being bitten by a Black Mamba. Even if they had boots and 4x4 vehicles – there would be a high chance that the victim of Black Mamba's bite wouldn't survive the car ride to the hospital. So, what could be done to ensure that didn't happen? They were instructed to keep anti-venom injections with them all the time and wear safety shoes that had to be worn up to a certain height. This would ensure that even if you got bitten, the shoes would prevent any real damage from taking place.

This had already put the workers on edge. It was bad enough that they had to navigate the wild to their jobs, but to actively look out for animals were capable of ending their lives in a single bite – it was horrible. Still, the workers all took two to four anti-venom injections in their side pockets or front pockets, praying they wouldn't have to use it. They had been instructed that in the event of a bite from the Black Mamba, they would have to administer the injection to themselves in their stomach. They were also warned that after that was done, they might lose consciousness for at least one...two...three hours. When you came back to your senses, you would feel tired, you would feel scared and lost, but after some time that feeling would pass. You would come back to being your normal self.

"This is reminding me of Afghanistan all over again," Karan thought, as he moved through his survey, keeping a sharp eye out for the Black Mamba.

Of course, a snake wasn't the same as avoiding landmines. The vision of the donkey being blown to smithereens had been stuck in his brain. But the anxiety of not knowing if they would ever make it out of there alive was something that was too familiar. His survival instincts had kicked in. Karan knew that if push came to shove, he would do everything by the book. He shuddered thinking about the snake.

While it wasn't big, it was small but had enough poison to kill a full-grown man within a few minutes! He and his men were wary of the threat that the small wild creature posed for them. Karan couldn't wait for this job to get over so that he could go home – home to safety – where no wild animals were plotting to take his life!

***

All this while, his profile had stayed active on the job portal. He received an inquiry from one of the top companies in India in his field, who reached out to him, impressed with his accomplishments.

"We came across your profile on portals, and you're a match to what we're currently looking for. We also noticed that you're based in Delhi – as mentioned in your CV. That's where we are located as well. We would love to interview you," the HR said, "Would it be possible for you to come down for the same?"

"If I did come down and don't end up getting the job," Karan reasoned, "I will be out of a lot of money, and no way to recuperate it. So, I am not comfortable with an in-person interview."

This was true. While he was making enough money to live comfortably, he didn't find it a wise investment to go back to India just for a job interview. There was no way to predict if a job interview would work out in his favour. If they decided to not hire him or go with someone else, he would be out of a lot of money – wouldn't really have the immediate means to recover it. Karan was honest and upfront about his decision. The HR took into consideration what he had said, and tried to find a balance between the candidate's and the employer's requests.

Since the HR knew he had chanced upon a good candidate came back with a counter-proposal immediately. "What if we set up a Skype meeting with our director for you? If you both want to work together – we can take it forward from there."

"That sounds good," Karan had replied. He was looking forward to this call. Truth be told, he was growing tired of always working for months on end from other countries and continents. He thought it was high time he settled into a nice office job.

A Skype call was set up around three days later, according to the schedule agreed on by both parties.

Karan waited in anticipation for the director to switch on his video, and he switched him on as well. It took them both a beat and then they realized simultaneously that they had worked before! The director on the other end of the line was one of his previous bosses. They both began to laugh at the strange turn of events.

"Oh, it's you, Karan," the director laughed, "I knew you were working abroad. And from your CV, I see you've added a number of impressive projects and countries to your list. I had no idea that we would meet each other like this again – especially over a Skype call."

"Me neither, Sir," Karan said, laughing. Fate really did like to play games at times.

"Well, if you're interested in his position, the job is yours. You can come down to Delhi, and join our company in a really good position. We'll ensure you become either the head of Delhi or the entire North region."

They spoke a little more to iron out the details of the deal. They offered him a really good salary as well, which Karan was more than happy to accept. To him, it seemed like a no-brainer. The time had come to hang up his wandering shoes and settle into an office job in Delhi so that he could be a present father to both his kids, and give them a stable and happy home.

This is what Karan had been wanting for a long time now. He had always hoped going back to work would mean he would eventually find a nice office job back home, and get to spend more time with his family. He could hardly believe his luck when it finally happened.

***

Karan didn't regret quitting his previous job and working in an office in Delhi. He had a number of really good projects in Delhi too. He finally made a subcontract that was around multi-million worth. He came into contact with a man named Mr. Umrao, who had the supplies to fulfil these contracts. Knowing that Mr. Umrao would be able to deliver, Karan gave him back-to-back contracts – all the projects that he had in Delhi.

Now, Karan had become the client, and Mr. Umrao was the contractor. They both got along really well. Perhaps it was his nature, or his work ethic – but something about Karan attracted Mr. Umrao towards him. He finally voiced what he had been thinking for quite some time.

"Mr. Karan," Mr. Umrao said, seriously, "How long are you planning to be in a job? Because at some point I think you should go into business. In fact, I think you should join me in my business. I'd love to make you a partner in my company – without any liabilities. Leave the multinational company that you are working in. I'll give you all the benefits they have been offering you too."

"Hmm," Karan said, in deep thought, "Well, you are right about that. I don't see myself working at a job for much longer. I would like to try my hand at business for sure. But can I get back to you in a couple of days?"

Mr. Umrao agreed, and Karan sought the advice of the one person who had been with him through thick and thin – Maata ji. Karan laid down all his cards on the table – about his contractor offering him a partnership in his business. Maata ji thought for a minute and said, "He's from Delhi, and we're also from Delhi – there's something to be said about these old ties. I agree with him, how long will be doing a job and working on someone else's time?"

"I like the life that has been set for us, Maata ji," Karan said, "Go to work in the morning, play with the kids in the evening. And sleep at night."

"Not really much of living that is, isn't it?" she asked, raising an eyebrow, "You're earning good money, but are you truly happy? This seems like a good opportunity and I think you will be good at it. In my opinion, Karan *beta*, you should accept the offer. It seems like the chance of a lifetime. You shouldn't turn it down."

On further reflection, Karan agreed with Maata ji. It wasn't going to be a financial risk for him. It would be a good way to see if he really wanted to be in business in the industry that he had come to love so much. He went to see Mr. Umrao a couple of days later at his home.

"I am ready to join your company," Karan declared, "But I do need three months to wrap up at my current job. After which, I am looking forward to seeing what we can achieve together."

Knowing that Mr. Umrao came from an influential family in one of Delhi's neighbourhoods and had the financial backing to help his business, Karan knew he was making the right choice. Once he came on board, they even got major projects together. Not only did they manage to complete the projects well, they did it well before time. The client was so thrilled with the results that not only did he pay them for the work done, but also gifted them an early completion of the project incentive.

Karan's fire had been ignited. He challenged Mr. Umrao to get them into the India Book of Records and Asian Book of Records. He achieved that dream by getting the fastest laying of sewer line – and got into the Indian Book of Records. Soon after, he got to enter the Asian Book of Records for a job well done. He couldn't have been happier. Everything was slowly falling into place.

***

During his work in India, Karan observed an unsettling reality: That few people in India were casteist. This realization disturbed Karan deeply. He had hoped that the professional environment would be free from such prejudices, but the reality was starkly different. Karan noticed that even in modern, literate circles, the remnants of the caste system were deeply entrenched. This was not just an occasional occurrence but a pervasive attitude that pervaded many aspects of life in India.

Karan had always believed in equality and the power of education to eliminate social evils. He was raised in an environment that valued human rights and justice. However, his experiences working in India began to challenge his idealistic views. People's casual comments and discriminatory behavior towards co-workers from lower castes were a stark reminder of the deep-rooted biases that still existed in society. Karan found it distressing that someone so educated and successful could harbor such regressive views.

One day, Karan found himself traveling to the interior parts of India. The bus he was on made a stop for a tea break at a local restaurant. The restaurant had a sign that read, "Those who order tea must clean their cup." It was owned by a Brahmin*, and this rule was strictly enforced. As Karan watched, every passenger on the bus dutifully cleaned their cups after drinking their tea.

Karan, however, refused to comply with this custom. He believed it was a manifestation of the caste system and was determined not to participate in it. The owner of the restaurant noticed Karan's refusal and confronted him. "You will not be allowed to get back on the bus until you clean your cup," he said angrily.

A heated argument ensued. The other passengers tried to persuade Karan to comply, explaining that it was simply the way things were done here. "This is a Brahmin-owned restaurant," they said. "He will not clean our cups, so we must do it ourselves."

Karan was taken aback. How could such outdated customs still persist in modern India? Instead of focusing on progress and education, people were still caught up in these archaic practices. His refusal to clean the cup was not just about the act itself but about what it represented. He could not bring himself to be complicit in a system that perpetuated discrimination and inequality.

In a moment of defiance, Karan grabbed the cup and hurled it against the wall, shattering it into pieces. The restaurant owner was furious. "How dare you break my cup!" he shouted.

Karan calmly asked, "What is the cost of the cup?"

"Twenty rupees," the owner replied.

Without hesitation, Karan handed over the money. "I will not be a part of your custom," he said firmly. "I refuse to clean a cup that I have paid for. I broke the cup to avoid being part of this discriminatory practice and to spare my fellow travelers from further inconvenience."

Brahmin – "Hindu priestly caste, traditionally scholars and religious leaders.*

The other passengers were silent, taken aback by Karan's bold stand. They had accepted the status quo for so long that they had never thought to question it. Karan's actions challenged their complacency and forced them to confront the injustice of the situation.

This incident was a turning point for Karan. It reinforced his belief that the caste system was a deep-seated problem that needed to be addressed. He realized that change would not come easily, but it was essential for the progress of society. Karan was determined to continue his fight against such discriminatory practices, no matter how difficult the path might be.

Karan's experience in India was a stark reminder of the reality that many in India still faced. Despite the advancements in technology and education, social progress lagged behind. The caste system, though officially abolished, still held sway in the minds and actions of many. It was a powerful force that perpetuated inequality and hindered the nation's development.

As Karan reflected on his experiences, he found himself recalling the words of Dr. B.R. Ambedkar, the principal architect of the Indian Constitution and a staunch advocate for the abolition of the caste system. Ambedkar had once said, "Caste is not just a division of labor, it is a division of laborers." This resonated deeply with Karan. The caste system was not just about social hierarchy; it was about the dehumanization of people based on their birth.

In one of his speeches, Karan quoted Mahatma Gandhi, who had said, "Be the change you wish to see in the world." Karan embodied this philosophy in his actions and words. He knew that change began with individuals taking a stand and challenging the status quo.

However, despite all his efforts and the progress he witnessed, Karan remained deeply troubled. He understood that the caste system was not something that could be eradicated overnight. It was a centuries-old institution, woven into the very fabric of society.

The road to true equality was long and fraught with obstacles.

Karan often found himself in a state of dilemma. He questioned whether his efforts were making a real impact or if they were just a drop in the ocean. The deeply entrenched nature of caste discrimination seemed overwhelming at times. He wondered how many more generations would have to suffer before true change could be achieved.

Yet, he also knew that giving up was not an option. Each small victory, each mind changed, and each individual empowered was a step towards a more just society. Karan was determined to continue his fight, inspired by the words of Dr. Ambedkar and Mahatma Gandhi. He believed in the power of perseverance and the importance of standing up for what is right.

Karan also realized that in our country, individuals often respect certain professionals without knowing their caste or religion. Doctors, army personnel, scholars, sportspersons, scientists, and other great personalities who contribute to the well-being of our nation are respected universally. Yet, in daily life, casteism rears its ugly.

***

Karan's son was in college for his second year, and his daughter was preparing for her Higher Secondary examinations. They had fallen into a smooth rhythm of life. He was enjoying his stint as a businessman, the kids were pursuing their education, and everyone was happy.

And sometimes, when everything seems to have found its place, something happens that shakes you up again. The remarriage portal that Karan had made in the hope of finding a life partner finally showed him a profile that interested him and sent him a message.

It was Miss Maya's profile!

He could hardly believe his eyes. It was the same Maya that he had liked a lot in college, but never approached her, knowing there was no future together. He had a crush on her almost twenty-three years ago. But to him, she still looked the same.

He remembered how he had thought about her randomly post his recovery, on a night when everything seemed bleak and hopeless to him. He had always wondered what would have happened between them. And now, to find her message in this inbox made his heart sing. He realized that all along what he had been seeking was seeking him! He couldn't wait to see how this particular story would unfold in his life.

On further inspection, he realized she had been divorced and was looking for her life partner on the remarriage portal as well. He explored her profile as much as he could and went through her bio-data as well. Then, he noticed that since both of them had paid profiles on the site, he had access to her mobile number. Before he could stop himself, he called her. She picked up after a couple of rings.

"Hello, Maya! Do you remember me? I'm Karan from Engineering College." He said, apprehensively.

"Hello, Karan from Engineering College. Of course, I remember you." Maya sounded surprised.

"You sent me a message on the remarriage site, didn't you realise it was me?"

"I didn't pay attention to your profile and just sent a text. Didn't realise it was you at all…also, forget the messages. Why don't you meet me in person?"

"Yes, that sounds like a good idea," Karan said, "Let's meet up soon."

He set up a meeting with her at the restaurant near his work. He smiled when he saw her. She still looked like the person he had liked so much in college.

"You're looking for remarriage, and so am I," Karan told her, earnestly, "And one thing I need to get off my chest – when we met in college – I used to like you so much. I can't express how much I wanted you even back then. But because I knew inter-faith marriages wouldn't work between us, I couldn't express myself at all. I thought there was no point in hurting the both of us, you know."

She smiled at his confession and said, "I understand. You should know, that back then, even I liked you a lot. But I couldn't do it either. I knew as well we wouldn't have a future together."

They both sat there, holding each other's gazes. Twenty-three ago, even going on a simple lunch date would have seemed like the end of the world for the both of them! it was a different world Karan and

Maya had grown up in, after all. It wasn't a tolerant world. It was a world that was constantly looking for excuses to set itself on fire.

Finally, Karan broke the silence and said, "Well, you messaged me on the remarriage portal. I accept. Let's get together then."

"Of course, that's just a wonderful idea," Maya said, enthusiastically.

Instantly, Maya's face lit up. She was beaming with happiness. She had liked his profile without realizing he was the same Karan she had gone to Karan with. She had definitely seen the potential between the two of them. Karan was happy too. He was glad he was getting another shot at sharing his life with a partner. He had waited for this day for a long time now. And to get Maya as the person who would become his better half – it was one of the best feelings in the world for him.

He got back to work for the second half, and couldn't wait to go home and share the good news with his mother-in-law. He knew she would offer good counsel and sound advice. She had remained by his side like a rock, and Karan had felt attachment and love towards her – as though she was his own mother.

***

"I think it's a very good idea, Karan beta," Maata ji said when Karan told her about Maya and the remarriage portal. "It's especially wonderful that you know each other from before. I think it's high time you found yourself a lovely life partner. You've already done more than enough for your family. You've made tons of sacrifices too. It's time for you to take some time for yourself. If Maya is making you happy – you should definitely marry her."

"Thank you, Maata ji," Karan said, gratefully. He had been a little apprehensive about sharing the news with her. Because as much as she had been like a mother to him – he was essentially replacing her daughter. But to have her understand why needed someone in his life and her giving her blessing to him – he felt relieved and happy about it.

Now that he had received blessings from Maata ji, Karan was feeling more confident about his decision. He couldn't wait to start a new chapter in his life. He was looking forward to having a life partner again – sharing his innermost thoughts, and looking forward to more lonely nights. He would finally get to have a chance to grow old with someone – something his wife's untimely death had robbed him of.

His children were doing well at the moment, and the business he had joined Mr. Umrao was thriving, it seemed like the perfect time to make a new addition to the family.

***

One night, before he could talk to his kids about Maya, the electricity current went out. The lights were gone, the fans weren't working, and the air conditioner didn't work in any of the rooms – except one – Karan's. His kids grew tired of the darkness and the heat.

136

"Papa, do something about this unbearable weather, please," his daughter pleaded.

"Why is it taking them so long to fix the problem?" his son complained.

"Ugh, I'm going to sleep in your room tonight, Papa," his daughter said, adamantly, "It's too hot and humid to sleep in our rooms."

"Me too," his son chimed in.

"Fine, fine," Karan laughed, "We'll make the beds and sleep like we used to when you were kids. Don't worry. I won't make you sleep without a fan or an air conditioner!"

They made their beds and slept off, enjoying the cool breeze from the air conditioner. Karan realized it was mostly a problem with the fuse and he wouldn't be able to get an electrician to come look at it, until the next day. He slept, peacefully, with his son and daughter on the big mattress.

When he got up in the middle of the night to go to the washroom, he noticed something that made his heart stop. Both his son and his daughter were sleeping peacefully in his room, oblivious to the change he was about to introduce into their lives. He sat down and kept staring at their peaceful faces. Right now, they were dependent on him and their nani. They could demand to sleep in the same room as him when they couldn't sleep in their own rooms. He would get married to Maya, and if the kids and her didn't get along, it would become another tragedy!

"Am I doing the right thing?" he wondered, "Is getting married again a good idea? Should I really marry Maya?"

What if they were too uncomfortable to voice their opinions on any matter? What if the kids got distracted by the new member of the family and forgot to concentrate on themselves? His son was in college, and his daughter was slowly stepping into young adulthood. It was the time she needed to be groomed the most. He couldn't take a gamble on his kids' happiness and peace of mind.

That's when he took another decision – he wouldn't get married again. Not to Maya or anyone else. His kids' needs trumped his own wants. He had lived long enough without a life partner. What was a few years more? He'd grown used to the idea of being by himself.

He never felt the need to tell his kids that he had almost married someone again. Or that he had felt lonely enough to want another life partner. To him, their safety and comfort came first. There was no way of knowing that they would have all gotten along well together. He couldn't take that risk. There were too many risks involved. He didn't feel prepared to take them.

When he was in college, he had thought that if Maya liked him, he would be the happiest person in the world. But years later when he finally got the chance to get together with her – he didn't find it as important anymore. At this point in life, his kids' happiness and well-being were more important to him. He realized that with time the importance of the things you want changes. He smiled at the sleeping faces of his kids. They slept on, blissfully unaware, that their mere presence had made their father choose a different option altogether and have a completely different life than the one he had been envisioning for a while now.

Besides, Karan told himself, life has been pretty interesting so far. What else is in store for me, I wonder?

***

It's been years since that fatal night when the cherubic faces of Karan's sleeping children steered him off the idea of getting married again. The company he joined with Mr. Umrao as a partner continues to thrive. His son is currently pursuing a master's degree in France, and his daughter is in college, pursuing her dream subject as well.

Karan kept his promise to himself and made sure his story had been written down. He knows that someone out there might use it as their survival guide.

All in all, Karan thought he had gone through a life that was well-lived and wanted to share the story of the same with the world. Because not every ending needs to be happy. Sometimes, just sometimes, the story simply just goes on. Maybe just not the way we have come to expect.

The Half Route:

Navigating the Unfinished Journey

In a world that constantly evolves, our desires, goals, and perspectives undergo transformation. Karan's decision to name his book "The Half Route" encapsulates this profound truth: our journeys are perpetually incomplete. The roads we traverse are filled with detours, unexpected turns, and unplanned stops. It is in this perpetual state of flux that we find the essence of our existence.

The Elusive Nature of Fulfilment

Reflecting on life's unpredictability, Karan realized that what we want rarely materializes exactly as we envisioned or when we envisioned it. The dreams we cherish at one stage of life often lose their luster as time progresses. Imagine yearning for something fervently, only to find it less appealing once achieved. This phenomenon speaks to the inherent changeability of human desires. Five, ten, or twenty years down the line, the things that once held immense value may seem trivial. Our appetites change, and so do the objects of our desires.

The metaphor of enjoying dry bread when hungry illustrates this beautifully. In moments of intense need, even the simplest sustenance becomes precious. Conversely, in times of abundance, we scarcely acknowledge it. Our changing desires mirror this cycle, highlighting the transient nature of human satisfaction.

The Inevitable Transformation of Self

The biggest secret of life is this: people change with time. They are no longer the people they once used to be. So, for better or worse, that was the case with Karan as well. At one point in his life, Maya had been important to him. But twenty years later, his children were more important than her. If he had to do it all over again, he'd still make the same choice.

This realization underscores a fundamental truth: our identities are not static. The Karan of two decades ago, who placed Maya at the center of his universe, evolved into a man who found deeper fulfillment in his love for his children. The decisions we make and the paths we choose are often reflections of our current selves, which are destined to change.

Embracing the Divine Plan

The biggest lesson Karan learned was that in the end, we are all part of God's plan. In the grand scheme of things, we are merely the puppets that Gods like to indulge themselves with. We come into this earth with our hopes, dreams, and desires – sometimes we're lucky enough to lead happy, nourishing, fulfilling lives. Other times, it isn't as good.

Life's unpredictability often leads to frustration and disillusionment. We meticulously craft our maps, plotting each step with precision, yet life frequently defies our plans. In these moments of uncertainty, it is essential to trust in a higher power. The divine plan, though inscrutable, operates with a wisdom beyond our comprehension.

Karan's journey teaches us that surrendering to this higher will bring solace. The illusion of control, while comforting, often leads to unnecessary strife. By accepting that we are part of a greater design, we can find peace in the midst of chaos.

The Illusion of Solitude

Orson Welles once said, "We live alone and we die alone. Everything else is just an illusion." This statement, though stark, carries a profound truth. Our lives, with all their connections and relationships, are ultimately individual journeys. Yet, this solitude is not devoid of meaning. The interactions and bonds we form along the way, though transient, enrich our paths and provide us with a sense of purpose.

In Karan's narrative, the illusion is not a denial of the connections we forge but a reminder of their temporary nature. The true essence lies in embracing these moments, cherishing the relationships, and finding meaning in the fleeting experiences.

Conclusion: The Beauty of the Half Route

Karan's philosophy of the "Half Route" is a call to embrace the unfinished journey. Life's beauty lies not in reaching a final destination but in the continuous process of becoming. As we navigate our paths, it is essential to recognize that fulfilment is not a fixed point but a dynamic, evolving experience.

In accepting the transient nature of desires, the inevitability of change, and the wisdom of a higher plan, we can find peace and purpose. The Half Route is a testament to the resilience of the human spirit, an acknowledgment that life's journey is beautifully incomplete, and a celebration of the ever-changing dance between our dreams and reality.

www.ingramcontent.com/pod-product-compliance
Lightning Source LLC
Chambersburg PA
CBHW021542150726

47990CB00006B/2354